Praise for Inga Simp

'Creepy and chilling, this becomes a hell-for-leather survival race through burning countryside'
THE OBSERVER

'A powerful narrative in Inga Simpson's unique voice. Horrifying, yet humane and ultimately hopeful – a masterwork'
ANGELA SLATTER

'*The Thinning* moves with the compressed momentum of a thriller towards a spectacular climax ... stunningly wrought'
THE GUARDIAN

'A controlled and literate work that earns its emotional peaks'
SATURDAY PAPER

'This novel is fast-paced, adrenalin-fuelled – and dramatic enough to keep me reading into the night'
ABC ONLINE

'Seat-of-your-pants gripping'
ARTSHUB

'Deeply affecting. Inga Simpson writes with literary brilliance ... action driven, intensely philosophical, a clever study of character and intensely beautiful'
LIVING ARTS CANBERRA

Also by Inga Simpson

Mr Wigg
Nest
Where the Trees Were
Understory
The Last Woman in the World
Willowman

For children
The Book of Australian Trees (with Alicia Rogerson)

THE THINNING

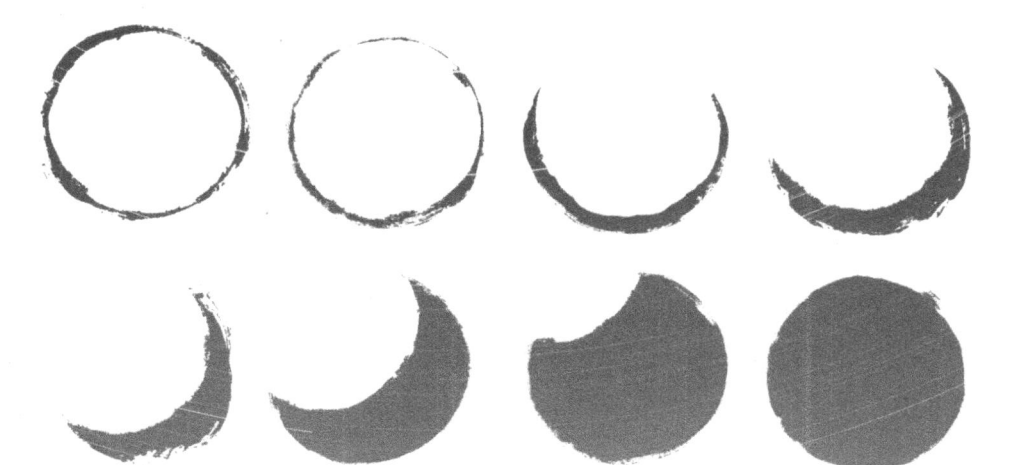

INGA SIMPSON

SPHERE

SPHERE

First published in Australia and New Zealand in 2024 by Hachette Australia
(an imprint of Hachette Australia Pty Limited)
First published in Great Britain in 2025 by Sphere

1 3 5 7 9 10 8 6 4 2

Copyright © Inga Simpson 2025
The moral right of the author has been asserted.

*All characters and events in this publication, other than those
clearly in the public domain, are fictitious and any resemblance
to real persons, living or dead, is purely coincidental.*

All rights reserved.
No part of this publication may be reproduced, stored in a
retrieval system, or transmitted, in any form or by any means, without
the prior permission in writing of the publisher, nor be otherwise circulated
in any form of binding or cover other than that in which it is published
and without a similar condition including this condition being
imposed on the subsequent purchaser.

A CIP catalogue record for this book
is available from the British Library.

ISBN 978-0-7515-7860-7

Printed and bound in Great Britain by
Clays Ltd, Elcograf S.p.A.

Papers used by Sphere are from well-managed forests
and other responsible sources.

MIX
Paper | Supporting
responsible forestry
FSC® C104740

Sphere
An imprint of
Little, Brown Book Group
Carmelite House
50 Victoria Embankment
London EC4Y 0DZ

The authorised representative
in the EEA is
Hachette Ireland
8 Castlecourt Centre
Dublin 15, D15 XTP3, Ireland
(email: info@hbgi.ie)

An Hachette UK Company
www.hachette.co.uk

www.littlebrown.co.uk

*Extinction always takes the form of an unravelling ...
that begins long before the death of the last individual
and continues to ripple out long afterwards.*

~ Thom van Dooren

These thin and sacred places wait for us to remember.

~ Kerri ní Dochartaigh

The darker the night, the brighter the stars.

~ Fyodor Dostoevsky

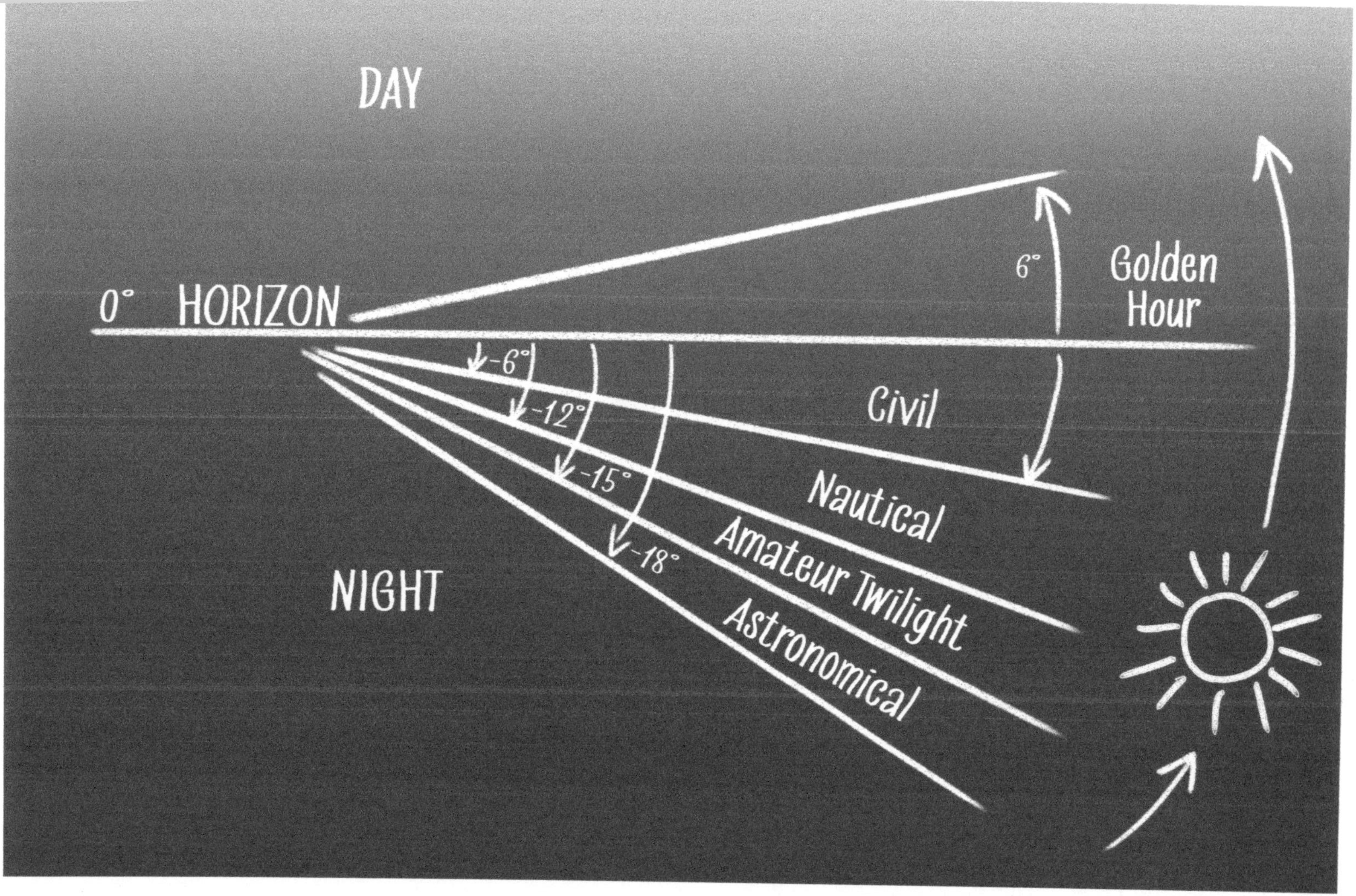
DAY
0°
HORIZON
6°
Golden Hour
-6°
-12°
-15°
-18°
Civil
Nautical
Amateur Twilight
Astronomical
NIGHT

DAY

Siding Spring Observatory

Gamilaraay Country

I LOWER MYSELF INTO the water. The rockpool is egg-shaped, washed smooth. The stream eddies around me before rushing away, down the mountain, clear and cold. My skin goosebumps and then calms. The immersion is a reset, opening my pores, heightening my awareness.

I shift my eyes towards the rustling in the fern fronds without moving my head. The tell-tale flashes of red, white spots on black: diamond firetails. They come to bathe at the spring. The water comes from deep underground, from the mountain's volcanic past, nourishing species still clinging to life. The firetails flit and whistle along the branch above my body, thin and tea-coloured beneath the surface. My fingers twitch, mimicking their movements.

'Hey,' I say.

They land at the pool's edge, exposing scarlet rumps as they dip and sip with matching beaks. The close encounter with another being sets a charge moving over my skin.

The shift comes before I register human noise, movement. The firetails dart off, into the undergrowth, taking the last of my body heat with them. When I look up, a strange face is peering down from the track above. The sort of face I haven't seen before. *Shit.*

I splash out onto the rock shelf and pull on underwear, socks and pants over damp skin, slip on my boots, wrestle my arms into my thermal, then my fleece, pull the hood over my head — and run.

My breath is loud in my ears. I head away from the spring, away from the path above, branches and leaves slapping against my cheeks and hands. I'm making way too much noise, leaving a trail, but I have to warn the others. When the undergrowth becomes too thick to push through, I climb the steep slope. So steep I have to dig in the toes of my boots and grip strappy lomandra to pull myself up.

At the top, I skirt around the cluster of white domes nestled in the bush. Where the trees thin, the undergrowth is easier to move through, but it's easier to be seen, too. I keep low and move fast, avoiding puddles and soft soil, leaping from tussock to tussock. Once the path firms and steepens, I run hard. My heart is pounding, the calming chill of the creek gone. I've messed everything up, for everyone.

When I reach the shoulder of the mountain, still in shadow, I drop down between two cypress pines to look back. Their sharp scent and furrowed trunks steady me. Three white vehicles, doors open. I'm too far away to read the numberplates or decals: MuX? Government? Military?

I turn my back on the scene, imprinting it to memory. I scramble over the mountain's shoulder and plunge down the other side. It's so steep, I have to zigzag to control my descent, slipping and sliding. With my vision blurred, smell takes over: callitris resin, damp soil, scat, wet fur. A rock wallaby startles, bounding away.

Deep in the gully, I leap from rock to rock to cross the creek and find the trailhead on the other side. The switchback climbs between cypress pines and ironbarks, into grasstrees and mossy boulders, leading me to the level clearing that holds our cabin. The two rooms, kitchenette and outdoor shower isn't much, but it has been home for these last months. I sprint the final distance, although I'm already spent.

Dianella is waiting in the doorway, boots on, body tense, her camera gear already packed. 'Heard you coming a mile off,' she says. 'What happened? Did I hear vehicles?'

'Three. Outside the lodge, near the main telescope. Four-wheel drives,' I say.

Dianella's forehead creases beneath her battered hat. 'Parks?'

I shake my head.

'You're sure?'

'I'm sure.' The flat affect, the pronounced eyes, had been unmistakeable. 'There's an Incomplete with them. Maybe twelve or fourteen years old.'

She's reading my face. 'A family then. What else?'

I drop my head. 'The Incomplete. They saw me.'

'How?'

It's a fair question. They say that Incompletes are short-sighted and ill-equipped for the outdoors. And I'm pretty much the opposite.

'I was swimming.'

Not one muscle in Dianella's face moves but her gaze sharpens to laser. 'Where?'

'At the spring.'

She tips her head in that pained way. 'How often have I told you not to go down there? And now, of all times …'

'I know,' I say. 'But there are firetails.'

I worry that if I stop paying attention, they'll go. And the water is my conduit to the heart of the mountain range, though I wouldn't say so out loud, even to my own mother.

Her face softens. 'How many?'

'Three. A breeding pair and a female from last season.'

'Oh.' She closes her eyes for a moment. 'That's wonderful. But you know we have to go now,' she says. 'Your bag's ready?'

'Yes.'

'I'll signal the others and meet you there. Don't forget the food. Two minutes.' She holds up two fingers, as if by making one mistake I've somehow lost the capacity to understand numbers.

We've done this drill a dozen times. In case someone came looking or one of us was spotted. I hoped it would never happen, and didn't even consider that it would be me. I take my spare outfit from the drawer and add it to my backpack, then the drybag containing the food, pull the drawstring tight, clip the buckles and sling the pack over my shoulders. Dianella carries the camera gear; I carry the food. That's the distribution of weight and responsibility.

I throw my collection of seedpods, leaves and feathers out the window, and watch them scatter on the breeze. The room is clean and bare, as if I was never there. I take one last look at the trunks and branches outside, the forest that has held me, and pull the timber shutters closed.

WE HAVEN'T ALWAYS LIVED on amber alert, ready to run. When Dianella was the astrophotographer in residence and Dad the head astronomer, we used to have a house, like regular people. By then astronomers could access the telescopes remotely and only needed to visit the observatory a handful of times a year, but the photographer had to live onsite. I woke every day to first light hitting the spires, domes, tors and plugs left behind by that great volcanic dreaming. The jagged ridgeline, unique in all the world, all the universe, which came to define my family and me.

Even before that, we used to visit the park in the school holidays. The first time my parents took me inside the main telescope, I fell under the spell of the clanking and creaking of turning machinery, the roof opening up to reveal the night sky, and those great lenses pointing out into the unknown. The retro dials, buttons, panels and screens of the control room were like a time machine. I never knew what I was going to see: a dwarf galaxy, the sulphurous surface of Io, or the Pillars of Creation within the Eagle Nebula. Sometimes we would link up with telescopes around the world and explore other galaxies.

We'd walk back to the lodge by red torchlight, the night calls of frogs, gliders and owls still loud. The vast web of the Milky Way was still bright, reflecting the peaks, valleys and rivers of Earth.

'As above, so below.' That's what Uncle Nate always says.

As I drifted in and out of sleep on the back seat during the drive back to Canberra, my parents would speak in whispers, the lines in their faces deeper in the green glow of the dashboard, about everything that was going or gone. Even in the park. That they needed to do more. Or that's when I think it started. Memories are like photographs, touched up and reprocessed every time we pull them out.

We had a whole community then, with other kids. And the observatory was our playground. After hours, once all the visitors had gone home, Jade, Pete and I rode our bikes around the roads and tracks between the telescopes and into the bush beyond. One summer holiday, we made a game of riding flat out at the boom gate. Whoever stopped first was chicken. As the youngest, that was usually me.

Until the evening when Jade didn't stop. She half-dismounted, ducked her head and shoulder, skidded her bike along the bitumen beneath the red and white bar, and somehow righted herself, whooping away down the hill. She must have been practising the manoeuvre for weeks, it was so professional.

When Pete tried to match her, thinking himself the superior athlete, he left half the skin from his left leg and arm behind on the bitumen. His parents, Stella and Dan, ran the visitor centre, and saw the whole thing as they were closing up. Jade and I crouched beside him, picking bits of gravel from raw flesh while Stella washed out the wounds with water. Pete didn't even whimper but he was the palest I'd ever seen him. We all felt better once Dan came back with the first-aid kit and covered up the red. They took Pete home in the back of the ute, like an animal found on the side of the road. Jade retrieved Pete's broken bike and we wheeled it between us, back to his place, as the sun set over the Western Plains.

The telescopes were characters in our play. Huntsman, with his array of telephoto lenses, like a giant spider's eyes, was to be avoided at all costs. Schmidt was a favourite, because it was out on its own and had been decommissioned, meaning our games were less likely to be observed.

We'd track the movements of staff and visiting astronomers from all over the world, constructing elaborate stories about spies, astronauts and time travel. We used to sneak inside, too, if the doors were left unlocked. Or even when they weren't. The time Jade found a complete set of keys lying on a coffee table in the lodge, we made a game of swapping around procedure manuals, pictures and other items. It was Dad who busted us, waiting inside StarTracker in the dark until we sneaked in with snacks and a thermos of hot chocolate spiked with rum from the visitor centre kitchen. 'You know better,' was all he said. And all he needed to say.

Jade and Pete were grounded for the rest of the holidays. My mother, after asking for every detail of the pranks, nodded as if in approval, then informed me that I would be cleaning all the telescopes 'from top to bottom'. I finished the work over four long days, winning my freedom, but had no one to share it with.

I hung out with Solaris instead, my favourite telescope. He's like a little white robot who sleeps all day. At night, his round head concertinas open and the telescope inside pops out. He's part of a network of Polish-owned telescopes searching for planets beyond our solar system that orbit binary stars – two-star systems – because they're more likely to support life.

I'd sit on his steps, reading a book. Or imagining the conversations between him and his sister telescopes in Argentina, South Africa and Poland. Or making up stories about all the lives I could live once I left home. I would study biology, ecology, or ornithology – anything but astronomy or photography – and save the world, all the plants and animals I'd grown up with.

Solaris is named after the science-fiction classic, not just because the author was Polish but because it was the first time a circumbinary planet appeared in literature. I put in a written request to study *Solaris* in English, but Ms Hartford said that we couldn't because the novel wasn't on the curriculum.

I did dream of being an astronaut. Sitting in the prime focus cage of the main telescope was a lot like flying a rocket ship, sailing through the stars, into infinity. Our technician, Blair, would move the telescope faster than he needed, to accentuate the feeling. Even walking around the catwalk inside the dome was like being in a spacecraft.

Other kids went to work with their parents, but they were in offices or out on properties during the day, not in outer space in the middle of the night. They didn't get to see what I saw.

As soon as we climbed the steps of the school bus on Monday morning, Jade was way too cool to talk to me. She lounged in the back seat, ruling her roost, while I read a book or watched something on my device on the hour-long journey into Dubbo. Pete was never like that, but he'd finished school by the time I went into year ten.

On school grounds, Jade ghosted me completely. Our double life worked fine until Hild, my bestie, got a crush and insisted we have lunch outside the senior common room, just to get a glimpse of Jade. Hild had left all her piercings in, even though it wasn't allowed on school grounds.

'Hot *and* aloof. It's an irresistible combination,' Hild said.

I rolled my eyes. It wasn't like I couldn't see it, but Jade is more like a sibling. And they were clearing trees along the street that day. The whine of chainsaws, the ripping apart of living fibres, and the impact of trunks and crowns slamming into the ground, was hard to block out.

Hild picked at her salad and kept looking at my chicken, lettuce and mayonnaise sandwich. I gave her half, as usual, and we watched the seniors skylarking, knowing it would be our turn next year. If Jade clocked us, she gave no sign. Her attention was on the alpha males sitting on the table in front of her, and probably their assessment schedule and the lead-up to exams. It was a lot of pressure, Jade said. Still, I envied their self-assurance and street clothes.

'Can't wait until we don't have to wear this stupid skirt,' I said.

'Or ask to go to the bathroom in class,' Hild said, 'like children.'

That's how small our concerns were, looking forward to little privileges, impatient for time to pass.

I LEAN MY PACK against a log on the edge of the firetrail and sit down to wait. I'm still scanning: the shift of the breeze on my cheek, the scurryings and scratchings behind me, a waft of pollen, the drone of a distant aircraft. Plan A, for a situation like this, is to scatter deeper into the park.

'A plan isn't a plan unless it's in place *before* the disaster,' Dad used to say. Usually in response to some government decision, or reactions, as he called them. Always 'Too late and too little.' We had plans, as a family and as individuals, for every eventuality – except for what actually happened.

I turn at the vibration, the movement in my peripheral vision. Our first group is on their way down the hill, clinging to tree shadow, their human shapes blurred by packs and all-weather clothing in muted colours. They're moving fast but each step is placed with care, to avoid dislodging a rock or grazing a boot. Dianella isn't with them.

I push down any worry. I know what she'll be doing: getting pictures of whatever is happening at the observatory.

Des spots me first and lifts his chin. He's Jade's dad, our local cultural astronomer and Dark Skies expert.

'Hey, Fin,' Jade says. Her hair has almost grown out, dark brown with just the tips bleached white.

I nod. 'See anything?'

'Four, maybe five adults. They're unloading gear, I think.'

'Maybe they're bringing astronomers back on site,' I say. 'For the eclipse.'

'The door to the big telescope was open,' Fran says. Her green hood is pinched in tight around her face, the same colour as her eyes. She and her daughter, May, walked all the way from Parkes during lockdown, when the Bill was passed. May was plump and clumsy when they showed up but is as lean as the rest of us now. I don't know what happened to May's other parent, if there was one, and I don't ask.

Blair and Uncle Nate arrive next. Uncle Nate was a ranger for National Parks. Still is, visiting the special places at the right time of year, caring for Country. From the moment I found the courage to formulate a question, I've been soaking up as much as I can about birds, animals, plants and all the backtrails. His eyes are smiley and he talks in the present tense, as if the current situation is temporary, which is easier to be around.

'We're heading up to Cathedral Arch,' Uncle Nate says. 'You and May want to come with us?' He's tying his hair up, making the question seem more casual than it is. Fran nods, relief on her face. You know you're safe with those guys. I watch Uncle Nate, hoping to glean his reasoning, but he turns away.

The otherworldly shapes on the way to the natural arch are like people turned to stone, beings frozen in time. It's one of those special places, where you can feel things that have happened in the past, where the membrane between our world and another is thin. A place where maybe you could step through, to the other side, if you knew how.

I can never get a straight answer from Uncle Nate. Des either. They always deflect the conversation somehow. It took me years to notice that. When I suggested that he was holding out on me, Uncle Nate just shrugged and said I hadn't asked the right questions. I still haven't, apparently.

The others come from the opposite direction: Dan, Stella and Pete. They're walking but at top speed, and even Pete, who made the state cross-country team, is out of breath.

Last to arrive is Dianella, running to catch up. Blair goes to meet her, leaning down to listen to what she's saying as they walk back. She throws out her left hand, the one not holding her camera. Blair's weathered face is grave, though he's trying to keep it neutral, and there is an intensity to their eye contact.

For a moment, we're all together again, embracing at the edge of the firetrail. I put myself in the middle of the huddle, gathering maximum body contact while I can. And hoping they'll forgive me.

'Well, isn't this a spanner in the works,' Des says. He shoots me a look that pierces my chest.

'C'mon, Des. We don't know who they are yet. Or if they'll tell anyone,' Dianella says. 'This needn't stop us.'

'She's put everything we've worked for at risk,' Des says.

'Enough,' Blair says. 'Finley knows she made a mistake.'

He, Des and Dianella step away and turn their backs. Blair hunches and puts an arm over each of them, as if taking them under his wings. They're talking in heated whispers and I can only catch snippets: what time was I seen; why an Incomplete; and how long should we wait to see if they report us.

I don't know what they're plotting, but before the observatory closed, Des and Blair were working on a project recycling space junk. 'Cleaning up,' Blair calls it. He says they could go further, if they wanted, and take out live satellites. We've all been living offgrid for months, but I know they still carry devices.

Uncle Nate steps between me and them. 'Hey, Finley. Ready to rock and roll?'

An image flashes, of him walking through two tall stones, his shoulders brushing both sides, and then disappearing – crossing over to where I cannot follow. My chest and throat tighten. It's another goodbye.

'Will I see you again?'

'Soon, I'd say.' He flashes me that grin which, for some reason, amid all that is going on, is the very thing that makes me want to cry. And then he's gone, leading the others away.

Dianella and I watch everyone disappear in different directions. They'll be headed for the old campsites, which have two main attractions: remoteness and water. Who goes where must have been decided ahead of time. Dianella doesn't share everything. She still doesn't trust me, even though I'm an adult now. But I don't need her to tell me where we're headed. I already know.

GOLDEN HOUR

Warrumbungle National Park

Gamilaraay Country

HURLEYS CAMP IS DIANELLA'S favourite. It has a view of Belougery Spire in first light on one side and last light on the other, giving her two full sessions in golden hour. On clear autumn nights, with the Milky Way arching overhead and a little moon glow turning the trachyte to gold, it made for an otherworldly shot. And that world was ours. Or so it seemed then.

Hurley is another thin place, where you can feel past, present and future all at once. It's the alignment of sun, moon and spire, and the long narrow gully with running water on both sides. Dianella's quest was always to capture it, convey its beauty. But it was magical long before she took photographs and processed them through three layers of software. What I want to know when I'm in those places is how to get closer, how to step through.

Maybe we did, some nights. While most people were asleep, and certainly most children, Dianella and I were out under the stars. My job was to paint light on the foreground with the laser and to keep an eye on the second camera. It's Dianella's practice to always have a backup, in case of battery or memory card malfunction. Camera B was never idle but running a long-exposure sequence or time-lapse recording, a secondary storyline on the same sky. The vision of Earth's rotation as the stars, planets and Milky Way passed by, cloudbanks coming and going, was mind-blowing. The first couple of hundred times, anyway.

Most photographers chase the light, but Dianella needs the dark. It is addictive. Just being out there, seeing a comet or the southern lights, is the most alive I've ever felt. And there is an alchemy to astrophotography. You have to use live view to get the settings right, but the screen on the back of the camera is pretty much black when you take the shot. Twenty or thirty seconds later, when the image appears, there are hundreds of thousands of stars and the dense swirling cloud of the Milky Way's galactic core is a physical, three-dimensional thing, with a full range of colour. In the dark, the camera sees so much more than the human eye.

It's like old-fashioned photography, Dianella says. When you had to develop rolls of film in a bath of toxic chemicals, not knowing what you had until the image began to appear.

The weird thing is that, once I saw what's up there in her photographs, I could perceive more with my own eyes. I don't know if it's my imagination filling in the gaps, or that the camera helped me to see.

Eventually I learned to set the interval timer and adjust the camera position to follow the galactic core. Dianella never said well done or thank you or even acknowledged my help. But sometimes she used the shots I took, which was as close to a compliment as I'm ever going to get.

Dianella scans in all directions while I squat down to put my ear to the bitumen, listening for a rumble or vibration. It's one of those conversations that we no longer need to have. My mother's lower back bothers her, from years of lugging heavy camera gear, and she believes I learn by doing.

Going to Hurleys means passing close by what was one of the park's public areas; this is an emotional decision.

'Clear,' I say. Life with Dianella has become such a military operation, she owes me a briefing. But I refuse to ask. I'm guessing we'll wait and see if anyone comes looking for us. We're less likely to be found in small groups.

We skirt the edge of the Camp Pincham carpark. Officially, it's closed, but I can smell the campfires and hear the low hum of human conversation. They'll be Illegals, like us. Down this end of the park, there are fewer sweep-throughs. They'll stay a few weeks and move on. Dad thought we should help everyone, share food and information. But Dianella says we need to keep to ourselves now. She doesn't trust anyone, and she has her reasons.

It's mean, but they'll be found first, if anyone does come looking.

We splash across the creek to break our scent trail and stop to listen again before stepping onto the smooth path. No drones, no vehicles, no lights, no heavy footsteps and, hopefully, no eyes on us. We're foxes, slinking along the edges, crisscrossing our tracks to obscure them.

Once we leave the main trail and make our way up the gully, I can relax into sensation: running water, damp air, croaking frogs, the high chirp of thornbills, the vibrations of crickets and katydids. The path is overgrown and the old timber bridge rickety. The water beneath stretches with the pull of the waxing moon, trunks and roots swell. We cross the meandering creek three times before we reach the little clearing. It isn't a place you could find easily, even in the day.

We drop our packs, roll out the tarp and inflate our thermarests. I lay our sleeping bags side by side, thin and lightweight but warm enough. All our gear is identical now. I've ended up taller but we're a similar build. The same curly hair, too, though hers has grown out grey.

The moon is only a few days off full – preparing herself for the total eclipse. Dianella hasn't told me where we're shooting yet, only that it's going to be 'spectacular'. It will probably involve climbing to some hard-to-access high point and rigging up the tripods somewhere precarious and uncomfortable.

Dianella sets up the cooker and screws on the gas bottle, humming some old song. 'You good?' she says.

'Fine,' I say. The lecture I was expecting hasn't come, at least.

I lay out the things to make a meal and a bag of salad from our garden. We've been growing what we can and killing feral goats for meat. Stella raised some goat kids and used their milk to make cheese and yoghurt. Dan, who did all the ordering for the visitor centre café, still has some way of procuring dry goods. Fran bakes bread and sometimes cakes in the camp oven. And Uncle Nate has been showing us how to gather what we can from the bush to supplement our supplies, flavour our food, and keep up our vitamin levels. Like wattleseed in our bread or warrigal greens from beside the creek instead of spinach.

Dianella cocks her head at a sound, an animal in the undergrowth. Probably a bandicoot. It's a good thing that they're still around, but she's on edge.

'No one's going to come up here tonight,' I say.

'True.' She slits the vacuum-sealed bag I hand her, empties the dehydrated goat bolognaise into the cooker lid, and pours water over it to soak.

'I'm sorry,' I say.

'I know,' she says.

I flick through the food packets again. We're only carrying enough for two days. I'm going to need more if we're climbing a mountain. So we're either meeting up with the others again or moving somewhere else. Like a safe house. Depending on what happens. Or maybe whatever they're planning and the eclipse are the same thing. It's all they've been talking about.

WE'RE SLIPPING INTO NAUTICAL twilight. It's the light sailors used to navigate, when the first stars appear but the land is still visible. For Dianella, it's just the time to set up, to prepare and frame her shots. But for me, this is where the magic is, when we're in between worlds.

In books or in school, when they talk about six degrees of separation, they mean connections between people. In our family, it means the sun dropping, six degrees at a time, in thirty-minute intervals: from golden hour into blue hour, through the three stages of twilight, until the sun is eighteen degrees below the horizon, leaving us in true astronomical dark – when galactic core visibility begins. That was when my parents' workday started and when the observatory came to life.

The whole process is reversed at the other end of the night, as Earth turns towards the sun, our day star. With all the evolutions through millennia, all the human impacts, the one thing that hasn't changed is that day always follows night.

I spot Sirius first, the Dog Star, which is closest, and moving closer. It's actually a binary star, two stars gravitationally bound together and orbiting around each other. I didn't believe it until I saw them for myself through the telescope.

Canopus, the navigator, is next brightest. Then the Crux and two pointers: Alpha and Beta Centauri. Beta is a *three*-star system. The two brightest are binaries, and the third orbits the other two.

But it's Betelgeuse, in Orion, who is brightest of all, even brighter than the moon. I call him Betel. We saw him go supernova, which puts you on familiar terms, even with a star. He doesn't drag on you, the way the moon does, but he has presence, just hanging there all red and spent, like my conscience. Reminding me why we're here and not lying on our beds in the cabin.

Halfway through astronomical darkness, when the centre of the sun reaches fifteen degrees below the horizon, used to be called amateur astronomical twilight, because most of the stars and constellations were visible without any high-end equipment. Naked eye astronomy, in other words, which First Nations peoples have been practising for tens of thousands of years.

Des says there have been supernovas before, which hung around for hundreds of years before fading. Cultural astronomy extends back long before written historical records, painting a bigger picture.

Dianella's eyes are on the sky, still appraising the best shot: calculating the time until Betel and the moon set, the shifting angle of the galactic core. Nothing is as straightforward as it used to be. Since the mining accident up there, the moon's cycles are all out of whack. And, with it, the tides on Earth, the migratory patterns of birds and other animals. Human rhythms, too.

We follow the sparkling burn of a meteor shower, debris falling to Earth, like all the species disappearing, all the words dropping out of the English language. If Betel exploding like that taught me anything, it's that nothing stays the same. Not even the stars.

Hurleys is named after one of Dianella's heroes. Frank Hurley was an official photographer for both world wars and Mawson's expedition to Antarctica. Dianella had one of his original prints hanging in her studio, signed and framed: a panorama of South Georgia Island with three masted sailing ships in the bay, the surrounding glaciers still intact. The photograph was a gift from her father, Vernon, a geologist and Olympic cross-country skier. He considered exploration and exercise equally noble pursuits, ideally in combination.

I never met my grandfather. He went missing on a solo expedition in Patagonia and his body was never found, like one of the stories in his old adventure books. Dianella doesn't talk about him much, but she kept all those books on the top shelf in her studio at the residence.

There was always something unsettled about my grandmother, as if she was still waiting for Vernon to walk in the door. She was kind, and baked cakes and slices when we visited, but her eyes never rested on you for long.

Dianella was their only child, too. Although she says he would have preferred a boy, to his credit, Vernon encouraged her interests. They paid for her science degree and then art school. It didn't matter what she did, as long as she aimed high. You don't get much higher than the stars.

Dianella documented the skies the way Hurley documented the wars and the ice. The last frontier, she used to call it. Of course, Hurley actually went to war, and Antarctica, whereas my mother hasn't been to space.

Where are the frontiers now? Is it even still a word? Sometimes I wonder what is left for me to discover.

'WHAT DID YOU SEE,' I say. 'When you went back.'

Dianella lights the cooker and boils water for pasta. The thinnest spaghetti, snapped in half, because it's quick.

'People moving in. A lot of specialised equipment. A sense of urgency. They've accessed the main telescope and SkyMapper.'

'Well,' I say. 'What does that mean? What's our plan?'

'For now, we wait.'

'For what?'

'For morning.' Dianella watches the sky for a moment and then shuts her eyes. 'Do you remember how it used to be?'

'The detail of the core and the volume of stars. Dark Emu. But maybe it's just from your photos.' It's not true. I often dream of the night sky I used to see. As if I'm flying through it.

In cultural astronomy, the space between the stars is as important as the stars themselves. Dark Emu is made of dark clouds of dust and gas visible against the Milky Way. His head is in the Coalsack Nebula, next to the Crux, with his body and legs trailing away into Scorpius. The stars and dust lanes of the Milky Way are Warrambool, Big River, and the spiralling galactic core is fire, its haze tendrils of smoke.

The stories Des and Uncle Nate shared brought the sky to life and connected it to our world on the ground. The Warrumbungles have always been a meeting place, where land meets sky. This always has been Dark Sky Country.

Dianella drains the pasta, puts the bolognaise over low heat, and stirs it with a plastic spoon, making sure she gets right into the corners, where it's inclined to stick and burn. When it's bubbling, she turns off the gas and turns to face me.

'Finley. You grew up beneath these stars. They're part of you.'

So are Dianella's images. The walls of our house, the fridge, our screens, were full of them. Geomagnetic storms stirring up airglow, crepuscular waves, ghostly zodiacal light from the sun reflecting on asteroid dust. Back then, Dianella was always smiling, even in the middle of a cold dark night on the side of some mountain. Especially on a cold dark night on the side of some mountain.

There was time then, to watch the world most people didn't see: Dark Emu flying through the sky, changing with the seasons. Dianella and I would wake up to dawn gilding Belougery. The Boulangerie, we used to call it. My parents still nostalgised about the travelling they did when they were young: French cheese, Swiss chocolate, German Riesling, taking an overnight train journey to the Cairngorms just to see ptarmigan in snow. The year Dianella worked at the Smithsonian or their dual contract with NASA. When I was little, I used to think they were made-up stories and places. Maybe I knew, somehow, that those things were already lost to me.

The picture that made Dianella famous was a composite, unusual for her. After years of painstakingly removing satellite tracks from her images in Lightroom, she decided to leave them in. The stacked picture showed all the satellite activity in a single night, the stitching across the sky that was sewing it shut. It was beautiful in its accidental design, the colours and shapes like a desert painting. It was Dianella's first big award, pushing the edges of technique at the time – and delivering a warning.

It was astronomers who came up with the term light pollution, when the gaslights of European cities first began to impair their observations. When Dianella's image went ballistic on socials, she used the opportunity to speak about the impacts of satellites on our Dark Skies. She worked with Astronomers Without Borders as part of the One Sky movement. First Nations astronomers from around the world were uniting to highlight the threat to their cultures. We were colonising space in the same way we once sailed ships to other countries and called it discovery.

The picture also made Dianella some enemies. For the big tech companies, she was a complication. First, they tried bribery: free cars, products, even space travel. Dianella refused it all. Then the threats started.

I was on my way home from school in Canberra's inner north, wondering why the oak leaves still weren't turning in May, when I sensed the dark van creeping along the street behind me. I snapped a picture, as if I was taking a selfie, then ran. I cut along the stormwater drain, into the community garden. Dianella looked up from her device as I was climbing over our back fence.

She applied for the job at the observatory the next day.

I'M CLINGING TO DREAM state, where there is no thinking, just sensing. Swimming with frogs, deep underwater, my back legs powerful and my skin reading oxygen levels, insect movement, other frogs. I'm drawn towards the light, bubbles clinging to my thighs, tingling and popping as I rise.

When I open my eyes, I'm breathing air.

My mother is already awake, propped up on one elbow. 'Hear them?'

'Pobblebonks?'

'It's a good sign,' Dianella says.

I unzip my sleeping bag enough to sit up, its warmth still about me. The sun has risen, though it has not yet reached our gully. Belougery is aglow, the early light muted and strange. Dianella sparks the cooker and waits for the water to come to the boil.

I watch her measure out tea leaves. We always had a pot at home, but it tastes better this way. I wriggle out of my sleeping bag, slip on my boots and walk down to the creek. The air is cool and damp, the water cold. I squat by the edge, rinsing my hands and wrists and washing my face. I refill the bladders from our packs and the water bottles, each movement slow and deliberate. The calm of birds and frogs and insects is all around, still carrying the feeling of my dream.

A crow lands on the branch overhead, their claws scritching into the bark.

'Hey,' I say. The crow tips their head to inspect me. Their beak and eyes are bigger than they used to be. I like crows, they're smart, but I don't take my eyes off them. In our school ground, they went all territorial, like magpies. Swooping and bigger beaks is a scary combination. But it's just the birds trying to adapt, evolution accelerating. Like shifting their habitats towards the poles or letting their colours fade as the rainforest disappears around them. Or the gannets, Dad's favourite seabird, who lost their photogenic blue eyes. The irises of those who made it through the avian flu all turned black, as if in mourning. Survivors are shapeshifters, they have to be.

Like the kid at the spring, who saw me. A new generation of humans is being born with larger eyes and sharper close vision, brains made for screens. People call them Incompletes because they cannot reproduce. Not with each other, anyway. With the fade-out of the Y chromosome and declining fertility rates, it looked like humans would join the Extinction List. Until they found out that Incompletes can reproduce with us 'Completes'. I don't know *how* they found that out. It's too gross to think about.

'Tea's ready,' Dianella says.

I hear it as I get to my feet. The *thwap, thwap, thwap* of a helicopter. Two, coming our way. And vehicles, in a convoy, from the west. Everything slows down and speeds up at the same time. I close the lid of the water bottle, turn and make eye contact with my mother across the clearing.

She drops into a crouch, head down. I mirror her. The helis fly above us, flattening the treetops, compressing the air. I want to put my hands over my ears, but don't dare move. I think they're headed for the campground but then they swing away, towards the observatory. It's been so long since we've been around so much noise that I'm struggling to think. *Focus.* One heli is larger, old-style, and the vehicles on the road are big, with lots of tyres.

Dianella takes two gulps of tea and hands me her mug. I drink what I can and flick the rest onto the ground. We pack up without speaking, methodical rather than hasty; it's quicker in the long run. Fold, roll, stuff, clip. The force of the attack, or whatever it is, seems disproportionate to the three vehicles that arrived only twenty-four hours ago, but they must be linked.

'What the hell is going on?' I say.

'I'm not sure,' Dianella says. 'But we'll regroup at Burbie.'

'Oh. Good to know,' I say.

'Pardon?'

'It's nice to know what the plan is,' I say. 'What if something happens to you? I won't even know how to find the others.'

'They'd find you.'

I shake my head. I'm still shaking it when I slip my pack over my shoulders and clip it tight. It feels heavier than it did yesterday, even though we've eaten some of the load.

'This isn't the time to get emotional,' Dianella says. 'It's to protect you. I'll explain on the way.'

I follow her along the narrow trail, negotiating each of the stream crossings and pausing to nod at the choir of greenhood orchids gathered in the damp. I catch up at the bridge and keep close as we head back onto the main track, glaring at the bright *Look Up* badge on Dianella's pack.

I try to focus on the running water, and to pick out individual birds within the chorus. But the smaller heli lifts off again, heading in our direction. It's not moving in a straight line but following the river or the road, getting closer and closer.

We step off the track, push into the scrub and crouch again. The new helis are electric and their range limited, but they're as manoeuvrable as wasps. And there's a vehicle approaching. One of the four-wheel drives, maybe.

The vehicle stops, close by. Doors open. The heli circles and drops lower and lower, then lands in a roaring blow of air. I'm trying to control my breathing but the roaring is inside my head, my chest. *I hate helicopters.*

My mother puts her hand on my shoulder, as if she knows I want to run. There are shouts, a burst of gunfire, so alien in the park. Then the heli is taking off again, swinging away to the north. The vehicle's doors do not close. It does not restart. All is quiet again, just a veil of dust hanging over the valley. It's over, whatever it was.

'You good?' Dianella says.

'Oh, I'm super,' I say.

'We can't use the road,' she says. 'And we don't want to be up on the Hightops. We'd be too visible. We'll backtrack, take West Spirey trail and cut across to Danu. Then follow the firetrail down to Burbie.'

I shrug. 'Whatever.' It's not like it was a question.

THERE ARE SO MANY images, sometimes it's difficult to separate them from our actual lives. The two that stand out are for my mother's reactions and what they foretold. The first was taken with a new camera on loan from the university, a two-hundred-and-seventy-degree panorama from Mount Woorut with the main telescope in the foreground. Dianella had planned it the year before, and the set up took hours, finding just the right position, and fitting in Solaris. That was for me. It was a clear autumn night, no moon, and we waited until the Milky Way was vaulting perfectly over the great dome.

I hung around in fleece, jacket and beanie, slapping my hands together and jumping up and down to stay warm. And then waited, motionless and silent, while Dianella took the seven frames in portrait mode, with a twenty percent overlap.

She never could wait until morning to process her pictures. I fell asleep on the floor of her studio while she was stitching the images together. It was the single expletive, which rarely escaped from Dianella's lips in those days, that woke me. I sat up, blinking at her screen. Even I knew what was wrong.

There was a glow at one edge of the picture. Had my mother made a mistake? Was the camera faulty?

'What is that?'

'The lights of Sydney.' Dianella's face, lit by her screen, was wet with tears. The city was five hundred kilometres away. Our Dark Sky Park was no longer dark.

My world was shaped by the stars, and the images of them, but most of all by my parents. I was their satellite. I didn't have words for it then, but my mother's grief was a weight moving into my body.

It was in that moment, that one wide-angle view, that I first understood that their world was diminishing. Our world. *The world.* That's the trouble with astrophotography and astronomy. All those powerful high-grade lenses showed us what was happening, what most other people didn't know or didn't want to believe. And once we'd seen it, we couldn't unsee it, couldn't unknow it. That was our family burden.

The second image was taken during golden hour. We were driving back from Parkes after dropping off one of Dianella's cameras for repair. And I was whinging about how much I hated the place.

'No one you speak to is actually from there,' I said. 'It's just a truck stop.'

That's when we saw the string of bright green lights low on the horizon, like the frontline of invading spacecraft. Dianella pulled over, tyres grinding into the gravel, and leapt out, leaving the car door wide open. She started setting up her camera gear, always at the ready in the back. I was still frozen in my seat.

'Call your father,' she said.

When he didn't answer, I left a message. After a few moments of staring, I climbed onto the bonnet and made a recording with Dianella's device. When the lights disappeared, we stood on the side of the road, double-decker road trains thundering past, wondering if it had really happened.

The images proved that it had. In the long-exposure shot, the lights appeared as a thin green line. The image went viral. Even the kids at school were talking about it. It was the start of the second generation of MuX satellites, the mega constellations being towed out, hundreds at time, to be deployed into orbit. So much for space belonging to no one. Everyone had signed up for cheap internet access, especially in remote areas like ours, because the big telcos still hadn't managed to give us proper service. This was the price.

If Dianella was an enemy of MuX before, now she was blocked at every turn. Her job and publication opportunities dried up, her articles online disappeared. Meanwhile, the southern hemisphere was fast going the way of the north, our stars fading from view.

She can't access her own pictures, all those decades of work. There are prints in books, galleries and archives. The original raw files are stored in databanks – and on the Cloud. But she can't go online to retrieve them or or log into any software to process new images, not without revealing herself and our location.

Dianella says she doesn't miss it. But she carries around a stack of memory cards and a portable drive inside a shockproof, waterproof case, like some sort of black box recording.

It's not just Dianella. Now none of us have ID, access to money, messaging or socials. We're shadow people, outside the system. And that's all because of me.

WE HEAD BACK DOWN the main trail, towards the carpark and the road, where the shots were fired. The paving is hard underfoot but allows us speed. We're almost at the fork, our turnoff, when something shifts behind the rocks. It's not goats; that's not the smell. Whatever it is whimpers, as if wounded. I move towards it on soft feet.

Dianella turns but does not slow. 'We need to keep going,' she says.

The sounds have stopped but I smell urine. Human. When I lean over the rocks, it's the Incomplete from the spring. They've pissed themself.

'How did you even get here?' I say. We're fifteen kilometres from the observatory by road.

The Incomplete tenses, as if expecting to be struck. Their eyes are large and pale behind glasses, and their convexity exaggerated. So strange to look into, and their face doesn't show much expression, yet I can tell they recognise me from the spring.

'Are you okay?' I say.

'They took them.' Their voice is so quiet and wavering, I have to lean in.

'What?'

'Mum and Dad.'

Dianella appears beside me. 'Are you hurt? We heard gunfire.'

They shake their head.

'*Who* took them?' I say.

'The soldiers. We were trying to get away.' The Incomplete is trying to cover the wet patch on their shorts. Their hair is dark and straight, a short, styled cut grown out. Of all the things that have happened in the park, this has to be the strangest.

'What soldiers? Ours?'

The kid shrugs their puny shoulders.

'What sort of uniforms were they wearing?' Dianella says.

'Black.'

I glance at Dianella. Our army doesn't wear black. Does it?

'What do your parents do?' Dianella says.

'They work for MuX. Worked.'

'Why didn't the soldiers take you?' I say.

'Mum and Dad led them away while I hid.'

'Did you tell anyone?' I say. 'When you saw me at the spring?'

'Just Mum and Dad.'

'And who did they tell?'

'No one.'

'Right. And then two helicopters just happen to turn up the next day,' I say. 'Let's go.'

'We can't just leave him,' Dianella says.

'What? We can't take them,' I say. 'They've got no gear, for a start.'

'We'll have to, and figure the rest out later,' she says.

I shake my head. *Whatever.*

'It's a long walk,' Dianella says. 'Just try to keep up.'

Another vehicle is approaching on the road. It slows at the entrance to the carpark. Two doors open. The kid is just standing there, panic-breathing.

'What's your name?' Dianella says.

'Terry.'

'Come on, Terry. Run!'

Dianella and I leap from sandstone block to sandstone block, working our way up the creek. I can hear Terry tripping and stumbling behind me, huffing and puffing. I stick close to Dianella, putting distance between me and the kid. The water burbling beneath my feet is the only thing keeping me functioning.

'You said you'd explain,' I say.

She looks over her shoulder and gestures at Terry. 'Later.'

It's a convenient excuse. Tree trunks rush by, a pardalote plucks bark fibres for their nest, a skink slinks under a rock. Life in the park goes on despite us.

As the path steepens, we give up trying to drag Terry along by the force of our will and check our pace. The kid is in shock, not just from the violence of whatever has happened to their parents, but from being left behind in what must seem like a hostile environment.

The sun is above us, already warm on our backs. We're exposed and moving too slow. I'm trying not to wish I hadn't stopped, trying not to resent Terry. But I already do.

DAD ALWAYS SAID BEING head astronomer just meant he got all the bad news ahead of time. Their work was already compromised by urban lighting and expanding gasfields. The telcos, superpowers, and aspiring nations kept sending up satellites which, in turn, was driving a new space race for precious metals. Universities and science agencies were reduced to minor players. The sun's rays reflecting off all those satellites was impeding astronomers' observations and images, and it was only going to get worse.

Dad tried to stay positive. He would stride around the observatory in an Akubra and button-up shirt, smiling and greeting everyone by name, stopping to chat. He proposed a series of new projects, drawing on the individual strengths of each team member, and our telescopes. He shepherded each proposal through the rigorous approval processes. The projects delivered results, too. His team's findings appeared in astronomers' journals and sometimes the socials, if there was a dramatic picture to go with it. Dad checked up on everyone and followed every development, problem-solving on the run. The place ran on his energy and enthusiasm.

He handled all the liaising with Canberra and protected the rest of the team from 'the political environment,' as he called it. Until he couldn't.

We lost the international Dark Sky rating first. Then the university's funding was cut, and Dad's team cut in half. He placed the letter requesting that he return to Canberra on the table during dinner.

'This came today.'

Dianella snatched it up. 'Oh,' she said. 'The nerve!'

I took the piece of paper from her, reading it twice to make sure I understood. I put down my fork and pushed my bowl away, my appetite gone. 'I'm not leaving the park,' I said. 'They can't make us. Can they?'

'*My* job is still here,' Dianella said. 'And our daughter is in the middle of first term.'

'I'll make the case for staying,' Dad said. 'Of course I will. But if things keep going this way, I'm not sure how much longer either of us will have jobs, Nelly.'

'Don't you dare start thinking like them. I won't tolerate it,' Dianella said.

Dad removed his glasses and covered his face with his hands.

'Can I please be excused?' I said.

Dad spent a whole day writing the reply. I listened to him reading it — and Dianella's edits — out loud. It worked. The university granted him a three-month reprieve. Dianella whooped, as if it was a great victory. But the university had its own reasons.

At first, we thought Dad's cough and weight loss were stress-related. But when they didn't go away, Dianella made him a doctor's appointment. There was a three-week wait for the medical centre in town. Even with a referral to the specialist in Parkes, he was on a waitlist. It was nearly a month before he went in for scans, blood tests and tissue samples.

Meanwhile, it was peak astro season. Dianella and I were analysing the weather forecasts, pollution levels and Milky Way viewing calendar, trying to find a clear night. We were hoping to camp up on Mount Wambelong, with the grass trees, to shoot the galactic core flaming from them.

Hild and I were studying for midyear exams. My room looked like a bomb had been dropped, piles of books and papers ordered by subject. We had English and maths together and got those exams out of the way in the first week. I packed two piles away, and shifted to science and geography.

Dianella drove Dad to Parkes for more scans while I was sitting my modern history exam. I was supposed to write three essays in the time but only got two finished. If I had ever understood the importance of the cold war, it left me in that frigid auditorium.

I was in bed but not asleep when my parents got home. They boiled the kettle and sat at the kitchen table, drinking tea.

A boobook called outside, low and deep, reverberating in my chest. Part of me did want to get up and ask questions. But Dianella's voice had softened so much, I was afraid I already knew the answers.

I failed my history exam, but they offered me a chance to sit it again or average my result with my assessment mark, which would still get me a solid credit. I was sitting on distinctions for everything else, so settled for that, given the circumstances.

Dad's test results were not good either. They came in the same Friday afternoon as the letter informing my parents that the university was pulling out. The Dark Sky Park was closing. His job would be transferred to Mount Stromlo Observatory, in Canberra, and the position of astrophotographer abolished.

This time we sat around the kitchen table together, a wine bottle empty in front of my parents, our meals unfinished, trying to comprehend the black hole stretching out before us.

After MuX purchased the observatory, they left a skeleton crew of one young technician and a caretaker to run all the telescopes. And they brought in their own, giving Blair and the others forty-five minutes to vacate the site before cancelling their logins. Most of the buildings were left empty.

The day the team of high-vis workers turned up in trucks to tear down the signs and dismantle the faded polystyrene planets lining the road in to the observatory marked the end of the final chapter of my childhood.

THE HELI IS WORKING over the park in a grid, moving closer. We burrow into the undergrowth. 'Keep your faces down,' Dianella says. 'Don't look up, whatever you do.'

I know it's for Terry's benefit, but it's irritating being treated like a child again. When the heli is directly overhead, the sound beyond bearable, I hold my breath and hope. How can they not see us? The trim on Terry's jacket is lurid red, his sneakers fluorescent orange. But the machine moves away.

'Do they know about us?' I say.

'Maybe.' She's chewing her lip and frowning, trying to fit the pieces together.

I glare at Terry. 'You're sure your parents didn't tell anyone?'

'Yes.'

The heli sweeps around.

'Should we leave the path?' I say. 'We don't want to lead them to the –'

Dianella holds up her hand.

'There are more of you?' Terry says.

Neither of us answer.

'You should just go. It's me they're after,' Terry says. Their forehead is creased, their mouth miserable.

'*You*? Why would they want you?' I say.

Dianella stares at Terry. 'Yes. Why?'

'To study me.'

Dianella and I make eye contact. What is the polite way to ask someone about their obvious genetic differences? For a moment I think we're going to hand them over, jettison the problem. And I feel less relieved than I thought I would.

Then Dianella pokes Terry in the chest. 'You're carrying a device.'

Terry takes a step backwards. 'Yes.'

'Get rid of it! Chuck it in the creek.'

We *so* should have checked.

'What if we tie it to something,' I say. 'And let it float downstream.'

'Brilliant,' Dianella says. 'Do it.'

Terry hands me the device, still warm from their pocket. I hesitate, taking in the high-definition screen featuring a weird cityscape, before I power it down, drop it in a drybag and seal it. Even now, someone else's glowing screen casts a spell.

I would never admit it to Dianella, but I do miss some of the apps. Like Stellarium, which allowed me to explore the night skies on my own, learning the names and stories of all the constellations and celestial bodies. And following the progress of *Voyager I* and *Voyager II*. It was comforting, somehow, getting those little updates: '*Voyager II* is twenty-five billion kilometres from Earth.'

While they're still out there, it's possible that the Golden Record they carry on board might be played millions of lightyears away, in thousands of years' time. The sounds we laid down, of whale song, birds, frogs, greetings in fifty-five languages, and images of pregnant women, human babies and cutting-edge astrophotography of the day seem naïve now, but they're a time capsule of human existence.

Mostly, I miss Hild. Just chatting and sharing pictures and interesting articles. Everyone needs one loyal and smart friend, and she was mine.

'Are you chipped?' Dianella says.

Terry pulls back their sleeve, exposing a healing wound. 'Mum took it out.'

I have to swallow hard to stop from throwing up. The cut is rough and will scar, but it's Hild I'm thinking of. What I left her to face alone.

I take the first-aid kit from the top of Dianella's pack and rip a strip of medical tape from the roll. Then I attach the sealed bag to a broad piece of stringybark. By the time I crouch by the creek's edge to set the raft in the water, the heli has moved north. We watch the device float across a pool, snag for a moment in the reeds, then drop over a ledge into whitewater.

Dianella's shoulders relax but Terry's face is distressed, as if they have lost a limb. And the only lifeline to their parents.

AT THE END OF year ten, I stayed at Hild's in Dubbo so I could go to the breakup parties. Everyone met up in the early hours down by the river, drunk and letting off steam. It had hit fifty-one that day, a new record, and we went skinny-dipping to cool off. It was an excuse for people to hook up, disappearing into the shadows.

For once, Hild wasn't among them, staying with me in the water until our skin was wrinkly. It bothered me that I couldn't see any stars. And what was I doing, out partying while Dad was sick at home?

The treatment was so brutal. He vomited for hours every time he got home and then slept all afternoon. My mother hardly slept, and all expression had gone from her face.

'It's just the booze talking, babes.' Hild's pale hair was flat on her head, the lights of the town glowing behind her. 'Let's get out – you're shivering.'

Hild and I lay on the bank, wrapped in our beach towels, talking about the following year, what we wanted from it. A relationship in her case. Rep hockey in mine. I'd made the squad that year but not the team that ran onto the field for the regional finals. I loved flicking the ball, guiding it to a teammate, and making an attacking move on goal. It was pushing myself, feeling the power in my body, being part of something. But I was one of four strikers, so unlikely to get a run unless someone was injured. You needed to be threatening in those positions, and I seemed to leave my confidence behind when I ran onto the field.

'You're fierce, babes,' Hild said. 'You just don't show it out there.'

I smiled in the dark. It was a good word. I pledged that I would be more fierce. And I told Hild she needed to be *less* fierce, and let the girls chase her rather than tackling them.

'You're exaggerating,' she said.

'Not much.'

We talked about when school was over, going to the same university, in Melbourne or Brisbane or Hobart. Somewhere far away, where we could make our own lives. Even if only one of us got a scholarship, we would share.

'Whatever it takes,' Hild said.

OGMA CAMP IS EMPTY but there are traces: a stump moved nearer the logs, a flattened patch of dirt where someone slept, the cypress switch used to sweep away bootprints, the faint track leading into the bush. Terry follows it, I assume to pee. Jade has left a round stone on a stump, like the signs she used to leave around the observatory. The creek is just a trickle, but the cool movement is a blessing. We sit in the shade of the black cypress and take in water. The presence of the others is still strong. All the animals and insects are on pause, waiting for us to leave again.

Dianella unties her laces and adjusts them.

'So. The plan …?' I say.

She reties her laces without looking up. 'We're working on a number of things. Trying to take back the observatory, for a start. But we might have missed our window.'

Terry steps into the campsite, shoulders hunched, face miserable. Their shorts have dried but walking with wet undies would chafe. The stink of it helps me squash down any sympathy. We refill the bladders from a pool in the creek, and a water bottle for Terry. Dianella places her worn broad-brimmed hat back on her head and leads us out.

I hang at the back, focusing on the changing country around us as we climb. We're heading west, passing Bluff Mountain, its shear face pockmarked with bright orange caves. I search for the peregrine falcons who used to inhabit them but nothing moves. The sky is hazy, as if a brown filter has been applied, and it's hot. This end of the park is drier and more exposed. Ragged rocky outcrops rise out of scrubby trees, lichenous rocks and dead pines bleached white, like old bones.

The heli changes direction in the distance. I wait until the others round a bend, drop my pack and crawl out to one of the high points Dianella has been avoiding. I remove my sunglasses and check my body and clothes for anything that might glint. All jewellery and piercings were left behind long ago, but buttons, zips and reflector strips can still give us away. I crawl out to the rock ledge beneath two ancient cypress pines, their trunks dark and solid, a gateway to the view out over the park.

The heli is searching southwest of the Parks' buildings. They must have picked up the signal from Terry's device. The main telescope is just a white pimple, high on the ridge, visible from almost everywhere in the park. With so much forest, so many steep hills and deep gorges, we could hide here forever, and just wait out whatever is going on beyond the park.

Our principal was emotional the day she made the announcement. Looking back, she had been kind all week, releasing me from a backlog of detentions and touching Hild on the shoulder in the corridor rather than barking at her to move, which should have been clues. The only other time we had seen Ms Lander like that was the day koalas went extinct.

We all had the daily Extinction Count running across the top of our screens. Some days the numbers turned over while you were watching. There might be an article or an image to go with it. So many sad little notifications that we went numb.

Ms Lander wasn't big on formality, but she called a whole-school assembly for koalas. We held a minute's silence, under the black shade cloth, which was one of the worst minutes of our lives up until that point. We couldn't look at each other. Even the death metal guys cried. It was so real for us. Koalas had been returned to the park, surviving wild in *our* forests. For a time. And then the last koala in the world, Minna, died in captivity at Dubbo Zoo, just down the road from the school.

So when Ms Lander called another whole-school assembly after lunch on a Wednesday, we were all in place early, waiting to hear what was so important. She climbed the stairs, holding her body very straight, and stood in front of the lectern. Something about her face was all wrong, twisted out of shape. She placed a single piece of paper down in front of her.

The Thinning

The other teachers leaned on the wall in the shade, hands in pockets or arms folded across their chests. We shuffled and shifted in the heat. Ms Lander looked out at us. Not over our heads, as usual, but at our faces.

She cleared her throat. 'I have an official announcement here that I am to read to you. About the Population Bill, which was passed late last night. I'm sure most of you have heard your parents talking about it, and how we got to this point. And I know many of you have been following the debates yourselves and expressing your views.'

She glanced at the piece of paper and then turned it over. 'But I'm not going to read that. Instead, I'm going to tell you what I have been asked to keep to myself.'

Hild made a noise, like a gasp. I reached for her hand and held it.

'From next month, mobile medical teams will visit all schools. All girls from year ten up will be called in for fertility testing, in order of date of birth. Oldest to youngest. Please understand, the testing is mandatory. And even I will not know what day they are coming.'

There was a moment of silence before girls started crying. My training buddy from hockey fainted. Our school captain, Dana McMannis, shook her head and mouthed *Fuck that*. Hild and I exchanged a fierce look that communicated we would never comply. We had learned all about feminists and revolutionaries in history; this was our time.

The guys fidgeted, trying to convey sympathy and hide their discomfort. A trans kid from our year stood there with palms splayed. If there was a caption, it would have read: WTF?

Ms Lander blinked away tears. For the first time, I saw her as a person. 'This legislation is directed at women and girls, but make no mistake, it affects all of us. In so many ways. Please, talk with your families. And, if you have questions, my door is open.' She crumpled the piece of paper into a ball and held it tight in her fist. The sun beat down on the quadrangle, as it had all day, but the quality of light had changed.

'Thank you,' Ms Lander said. 'All students, please return to class.'

Hild and I skipped maths, hiding out in the cool of the library. It made such awful sense; school was compulsory, and people were all grouped together, which was more efficient, especially in remote areas.

'This is about the Incompletes?'

Hild nodded. 'The first generation are reaching maturity. But they need our eggs. Do you know how intrusive those tests are?'

I didn't. But trying to imagine was making me nauseous. 'And then what happens?'

'Exactly. We have no idea.' Hild was trying to whisper but we were full of rage.

I pretended to scan the index of a reference book as the librarian stalked past, narrowing his eyes. It wasn't the first time we'd skipped class in the stacks. And we didn't know what the other teachers thought of what Ms Lander had done.

'From now on, we only trust each other,' I said.

'Agreed.'

I started drawing up a list. 'Step one, talk to the parentals.'

Hild nodded. 'Whatever happens, we'll deal with it together. Even if it means we have to run away.'

WHERE THE TRAIL CROSSES an exposed spill of scree, Terry sends a rock tumbling, startling a family of goats in all shades of shaggy wool. They crash off into the undergrowth, which sets more rocks clattering down the slope. We freeze, waiting for the noise to settle, listening for a response.

When none comes, Dianella and I make our way to the other side and wait while Terry picks their way arounds stones and thistles, slower than I thought possible.

Dianella smiles and encourages them, suddenly all patience.

I roll my eyes.

'I saw that,' she says. Her smile is gone.

We settle into a rhythm: Dianella leading, Terry in the middle, me bringing up the rear. It's painful watching Terry struggling to navigate the terrain, flinching at the slightest touch of a leaf or insect, but less irritating than hearing that huffing and whimpering behind me. And it leaves more room for my own thoughts.

Dad picked me up from the school bus that day. He was there waiting, leaning on the car, beanie over his bald head. Ms Lander had phoned all the senior girls' parents. Even as Dad hugged me, and I felt his ribs beneath his fleece, I was wondering how Ms Lander would explain to the people from Health, when they arrived, why there were so many of us missing.

'Crap day, huh?' Dad said.

I nodded.

His hands were pale and thin on the steering wheel as we wound up the mountain. Everything was where it had been when I left that morning but nothing was the same.

We sat around the kitchen table with a pot of tea and three slices of pumpkin spice cake but no one touched it.

'The first thing to say is that we don't agree with any of this,' Dad said.

'The results will be on record forever,' my mother said. 'From there, it's a slippery slope. Next they'll be harvesting eggs.'

Dad turned his cup around in its saucer. 'The new legislation allows Health to compel people to –'

'Hild and I have already talked about it. We won't do it. No way.'

Dad and Dianella looked at each other over the table.

'What?' I said.

'Hild's parents are high up in that department. I don't see how they can make an exception for their own daughter,' Dianella said.

'They'll have to quit,' I said.

'It's not that simple.' Dad coughed and drew a ragged breath. 'Even for us. To get you out of this, we'll all have to disappear. We'll have to leave everything behind.'

'But we can take Hild,' I said.

Again, my parents just looked at each other.

'What? You love Hild!'

My mother made a noise in her throat.

Dad put his hand on my forearm. 'If Hild wants to come with us, she can,' he said.

Where clearwater flows over coloured stones, I stop to drink, taking a trickle of mountain inside me. The grasstrees whisper, the breeze shifting their fronds, like long-haired people.

'Hey,' I say.

Behind us, the sun is on the broad back of Bluff Mountain, sloping away towards the Western Plains.

We're approaching the trailhead to Cathedral Arch. Uncle Nate and Blair will be long gone, but I can feel the outer edge of the magic of that place, the call into another dimension, where none of this is happening. Where I didn't swim at the spring and forget myself for one moment too long. Then Terry wouldn't be our problem.

Dianella and I spent a night up at the arch once. She captured incredible footage of the stars moving above the ramparts on the ridge, and the weird shadows cast by the rock people.

A strange sighing wind circled us. Neither of us could sleep. When I kept shifting in my sleeping bag, Dianella put her arm over me, as if I was afraid. But it was more that the energy was so wild. And when I did sleep, my dreams were wild, too. Of flying among stars and bright matter, but falling back to Earth.

Dianella never published those images. 'It doesn't feel right,' she said.

The shot we took of the gum tree growing out of the natural stone arch, arched in turn by the Milky Way, was the only one she printed.

I shut my eyes to recall the feeling of the place. But it's Dad who comes to mind. The way he used to say, 'Beam me up, Scotty,' as he pushed back his glasses, whenever he was drowning in uni administrivia. I used to groan at all those old sci-fi screen references but I watched every daggy episode while he was sick.

When I catch up to the others again, Dianella fussing over Terry, touching their skinny shoulders, offering water, as if her parenting gene has kicked in again, is too much. I hang back, just close enough to keep them in sight.

AS SOON AS I saw Hild's face the next day, I knew.

Some girls were already missing, and all the trans crowd. It was like the clock had been wound back, and identity was up for debate all over again. The whole school was unsettled, patterns and habits broken. The pale brick buildings didn't even look the same.

Hild and I hugged in the orange foyer of the senior common room.

'Hey,' Hild said. But she didn't smile.

'What's happened?'

'Mum needs to be seen to be setting an example, basically.'

'Can't she get another job?'

'Not with the downturn ... They say it won't be that bad. It's just testing.'

'And keeping our results on file.'

Hild glanced around the room. 'You know I agree with you.'

'Was your mum part of this policy?'

'She was against it.' Hild picked at her nails. 'But I guess we have to do something, if humans are going to survive.'

The common room was filling up. And with it, the stink of adrenaline-heavy sweat. Other girls pulled blue plastic chairs together in close huddles, talking in low tones. The sudden return to a gender divide left the boys uncertain, trying to relieve the tension by kicking a golf ball towards an imaginary goal line on the worn grey carpet. Mal Harding, who I'd dated during year nine, was laughing too loud, playing the joker. He was smarter than that, I knew, though he hid it well.

Someone had graffitied the diversity poster, spraying male and female symbols in fluorescent green over the kids' faces. The helpline QR codes had been scribbled out with a black sharpie. We were on the peak of a wave that was already breaking.

'Come with us, Hild. Please?'

'I can't do it to Mum and Dad,' she said. 'And I do want to finish school. That's important. What about all our plans, going to uni?'

I looked away, over the concrete quadrangle, blinking back tears. 'I think those plans are out the window, either way.'

༄

We don't stop until we reach Danu, on the saddle at the base of Mount Wambelong. I scramble up to the top of the rock near the tent site, standing alone there, while Dianella treats some bite or scratch on Terry's scrawny little leg. The bare plains shimmer in the heat. Scrubby wattle regrowth crowds up around dead branches. Tucked in behind the ridgeline, we have no view back to the observatory and the heli is just a distant noise.

The currawong who always seems to be at the old campsite lands on the rock next to me.

'We've got nothing for you,' I say. She's an old-school bird, normal beak and eyes, which are looking right back at me. My skin and scalp tingle. If I could speak their language, I'd ask how far ahead the others are. But there are probably better questions. Like, what do you see? And what is coming next?

Currawong glides down to the others, inspecting Dianella and then Terry, who shifts away. They take a little bottle from their pocket, and remove their glasses to put drops in their eyes. Such a vulnerable creature. Like one of those pale cave fish, thrown out of the water.

Wambelong looms in front of us, and the signed trailhead up to the summit. It's my favourite walk in the park, climbing the outer slopes of the volcano through great stands of ancient grasstrees. They are definitely beings, with a wisdom you can feel, especially when gathered in large groups.

'Right. Let's move out,' Dianella says. She makes a dramatic arm motion, setting our direction. I climb down, my feet sure and true. The breeze is fresh, ripping up the firetrail from the south. We're on the way to rest, food and answers. And getting rid of Terry.

The firetrail is steep and the gravel loose, but it's downhill, at least. Or mostly downhill. The road has been built into a series of rises and falls to prevent erosion. Even I'm puffing on the ups. Terry is slipping and sliding, sniffing back tears.

Dianella stops again, to let Terry get their breath, drink, and to pour water over their wrists to cool their core temperature, which seems inclined to shoot up at sharp angles, turning their cheeks and nose pink.

We could be there by now.

I glance back at Wambelong's peak, where the grasstrees are in conference. The first time I summited was with Dad, a few weeks after we moved. It was not the fine day that had been forecast but cold and windy. We were hunkered into our fleeces, waterproofs and beanies, peering out over the edge at the park below, when the wedge-tailed eagle rose up, levitating like some kind of god, and just held there, huge, on the updraft, turning her eyes on us. She was so close I could have touched her wingtips. Dad grabbed my arm and we stood, grinning like idiots into the wind.

When we got home, Dianella said that we were 'off our faces'. And we kind of were, I guess, on the experience.

DAD'S ILLNESS GAVE ME a way out. My mother handwrote a letter to the deputy principal – who was acting principal while Ms Lander was 'on leave' – informing him that she was taking me out of school for the rest of term while she cared for Dad. By then, Dianella didn't trust the school messaging service. She photographed the letter, then sealed it inside an envelope and handed it to me. I was to deliver it in person.

On the bus that day, I didn't read or listen to music like I usually would. I just stared out the window, taking in every detail: yet another lane on the highway going in, more high-density housing estates. The driverless vehicles that freaked me out, especially the B-triples hauling pink plastic-wrapped cotton bales, like giant caterpillars on the loose. The other kids were talking and laughing behind me as if everything was completely fine.

If the teachers noticed that I was checking out, they let me go. With the strikes, most of our classes were unsupervised. Expecting us to be self-motivated with everything that was going on wasn't exactly realistic.

That lunchtime, Hild and I went down to the grassy bank beside the row of casuarinas and took off our shoes and socks. We had our novels but didn't open them. I'd been carrying around the third book from Dad's favourite Scandinavian detective series for weeks, unable to focus for more than a page or two at a time. Hild was reading the set text for English: *Emma*. I hadn't even bothered picking up a copy from the box on Ms Hartford's desk. I wouldn't be going back to English and didn't see much room for Jane Austen in my life.

Hild and I were still close, but now there were things that went unsaid, topics we avoided. We split my sandwiches and Hild's salad, as usual. I had brought a thermos and two slices of my mother's lemon myrtle tea cake. Hild teared up as soon as she saw it. I think she knew then that it was my last day.

'Oh my god,' she said. 'I fucking love this cake.'

'Dianella made it for you,' I said, handing over one of the slices and a little bamboo fork. If I had ever told her how much butter and sugar was in that cake, she would never have eaten it. That day, we savoured every moist crumb and licked our forks clean. I had visual arts in the afternoon while she had music, and then a maths tutoring session when I had to catch the bus. Not knowing when we would see each other again weighed heavy.

'How's your dad?' she said.

I shook my head. 'He has to go to that hospital in Parkes. The silicosis is manageable. Sort of. But now they've found secondary tumours. They'll try to get them but ...'

'I'm so sorry, babes.'

'I don't know what to do anymore.'

She put her arms around me, there on the edge of the school oval, noisy miners squawking above us, the buzz and chatter of students fading into the distance. When the bell rang, I didn't want her to let go.

I TAKE THE LEAD for the final leg, sticking to the shady side of the trail. The descent is so steep, my quads are burning. I'm grateful for a short uphill stretch – until my heart is pounding so hard, I'm longing for downhill again. It's the sort of walk where I'm focused on the destination, on it being over. Terry is red in the face, struggling to put one foot in front of the other. Dianella looks no different. Her energy changes but never dims.

A hint of a breeze finds us. At last, I see the broad clearing that is Camp Burbie. Uncle Nate is filling a water bottle at the tap. Blair and Des are sitting opposite each other on broad logs, elbows on knees, in deep conversation. Stella and Fran are preparing a meal. Pete and Dan are trying to keep May distracted in the shade. Jade is reorganising her pack, the contents spread out over her groundsheet, her arms buff in a khaki singlet.

An eastern yellow robin welcomes us, darting down to take a grub and returning to the tree trunk, clinging on firm feet. I can almost taste the grub's nuttiness, the grits of dirt.

Uncle Nate turns, raises one arm high in greeting. His grin fades into something more quizzical when he sees Terry. Then everyone else turns and stares. I can feel Terry squirming.

We drop our packs at the end of the logs and they gather around us, slapping arms and shoulders.

Jade hugs me first. 'We were worried, with the helis.'

'Nah,' I say. 'We outsmarted them.'

'Everybody, this is Terry,' Dianella says. 'A small force turned up at the observatory this morning and took Terry's parents. And now that heli is looking for Terry.'

'What force?' Des says.

'Why?' Blair says.

Fran looks up from the bowls she's laying out. 'So they're not looking for us?'

Everyone is speaking at once and no one is listening. Terry steps back, almost falling over the log.

'We need to have a proper meeting,' Dianella says.

'Not before we eat,' Stella says. 'Lunch is ready. And you know my policy: no business with food. Fin, Terry, get yourselves cleaned up and give me a hand.'

WE HAVE NO FIRE to focus on, just food laid out on a stump. Fran has made flatbread in a pan on the cooker. There is oil and a wattleseed dukkha to dip it in. And goat curry with basmati rice and a side of steamed warrigal greens, mango chutney and yoghurt. I pile my plate high. Terry, ridiculous in a pair of Pete's shorts, takes modest portions of everything and perches next to me. Though not before carefully checking the log and the ground beneath their feet. Jade sits opposite, her plate nearly as full as mine.

'Where did you camp?'

'Hurley,' I say.

She nods. 'Knew it.'

'How close did the heli come?'

'It flew right over,' Jade says. 'But we hadn't started setting up.'

We shovel food into our mouths, making appreciative noises. Food is just fuel when you're on the trail but the fuel may as well taste good. Fran used to have a café in Parkes, the kind that people drive out from the city for.

I tune in to the yellow robin, still calling from the shadows on the edge of the clearing. They are so insistent, like a recurring thought. The angle of their heads when they peer down at the ground from the side of a tree trunk is so imprinted on me that I can't help leaning forward as I imagine their movement.

I mop up the last of the curry with the bread, wishing I had savoured everything a little longer. But I'm ready to get the meeting done, so we can figure out what is happening and start whatever is next.

Blair lights the cookers and gets water on the boil. Tea is a tradition, the oil that runs their machine. Blair likes his cup full, not low tide, and the tea strong but not stewed. I learned that the hard way, sent back to remake it more than once. Which is a big deal if you've carried in all your water. Half the time he doesn't even drink it all, but he makes better decisions with tea, he says. That's how I always picture him, nursing a camp mug in his strong hands.

Stella hands around a block of dark chocolate. Her fringe doesn't cover the worry in her eyes. I snap off a whole row and hand the block to Terry, who rustles the packaging more than seems possible. I close my eyes and chew one square at a time.

'Okay, Terry,' Dianella says. 'Will you please share what you saw?'

Terry flushes red and takes an exaggerated breath. 'We were in the car when the soldiers came. Mum drove out, before the boom gate closed. And then they chased us down the mountain.'

'What were your parents doing at the observatory?' Des says.

'Installing new software they'd developed. They're satellite security specialists. They were –'

Dianella leans forward. 'Why were you in the car already? Did you know they were coming?'

'There was a NASA team due in a few days as part of the same project. They had been asking questions. About me,' Terry says. 'Too many questions. My parents planned to disappear before they arrived.'

'NASA?' I say.

Des frowns. 'Why is NASA interested in Incompletes?'

Terry turns those bulging eyes on Dianella, as if for help. But she says nothing.

Blair sips his tea. 'Do you know anything about this security software, Terry?'

'Um. Something to do with a docking plate,' Terry says.

Des and Blair exchange a look.

Uncle Nate has just been listening and watching Terry. 'Your parents didn't tell anyone about Finley, did they?'

'They wouldn't,' Terry says. 'We were about to go on the run, too. It would have drawn attention to us.'

'Where were you going to go?' Blair says.

'Queensland,' Terry says.

Des rubs his chin, glints of silver in the stubble. 'This still fucks everything up.'

'Maybe it doesn't,' Blair says.

'How many of these soldiers did you see?' Jade says.

'Twelve.'

Jade nods, as if she's considering taking them on.

'What will happen to my parents?' Terry says.

Blair uncrosses his legs. 'We'll try to find out. And, in the meantime, we'll keep you safe.'

The meeting is over. Terry and I are dismissed.

I WALK ACROSS TO the tap to fill the cookers with water. I get Terry being kept out of the decision-making, but I grew up in the park. I know it as well as anyone. And I'm no babysitter. Fairy wrens work over the ground for crumbs, all in the dull brown plumage and pale blue tails of females. But come spring, some of them will transition to bright male colours.

I boil water to wash up, rinsing the plates in dirty water first and then scrubbing them clean, propping them upside down to dry.

'May,' I say. 'Wipe up for me?'

She catches the tea-towel I throw her and finds another for Terry.

Dianella has rolled up her shirtsleeves, exposing lean brown arms, ready for action. Uncle Nate, Des and Blair are sitting close, in animated conversation.

I start on the pots and pans, the deep yellow of the curry staining the water. May packs things away while Terry does a decent job of wiping.

'You did that at home?' I say.

'Yes,' they say. 'After dinner.'

May hangs the tea-towels and cloth from a branch to dry. I pack up the cookers and tuck the little detergent bottle inside Fran's kit. Maybe she'll take Terry. Or maybe Dan can get Terry out, to one of the safehouses.

Terry is fidgeting.

At least from here on, I can walk with Uncle Nate or Jade instead.

'Fin?' Terry touches my bare forearm. I don't mean to, but I flinch. Their head drops. The worst part is that Terry expects it, but for a moment, they forgot.

I soften my voice. 'What is it?'

'What if I need to …'

'There's a shovel on top of the sign near the water tap,' I say. 'Dig a hole and squat over it. Do your business. Cover it over again. Easy. Just make sure the hole is a foot deep and that you're at least a hundred metres from camp.'

The kid looks at me as if it is the worst horror imaginable. But it must be urgent because Terry hurries away, across the clearing. When they struggle to remove the shovel from its roost, I don't get up to help.

Terry returns to the tap, stows the shovel and washes their hands over and over. I watch the birds, mimicking the flit of the wren's tail with my forefinger, trying to summon a calm and patience that I do not feel.

They make their way across the clearing and stand between me and the sun. 'It says not to drink that water unless you boil it, but you filled our water bottles there.'

'It's rainwater. Fresh as. They said that at every campsite to cover their arses.'

I cannot wait to be rid of Terry's whining. But I do feel bad. I'm being a bitch and their parents have just been kidnapped.

May is playing at my feet and keeps glancing at Terry. She's just curious, but it's obvious.

'Why don't you do a loop around the campground,' I say. 'Check for any rubbish. Even a speck. We have to leave this place perfect.'

She runs off, working the circle clockwise.

'Your parents are scientists?'

'Dad's an information engineer. Mum's the astronomer.'

'Cosmologist?'

'Yes.'

'So was my dad.'

'Every astronomer in the world knows who your father was,' Terry says.

I can't help but smile. It's easy to forget when you see someone every day. *Saw.* Dad discovered one big thing in his late twenties: traces of one of the first stars in the universe, inside another ancient star. It was a time machine taking us right back to the origin stars. Those blue giants are all gone now but we could learn about them through their offspring. And that second-generation star turned out to be rare, anaemic, with the lowest iron levels ever recorded.

People expected Dad to make a string of discoveries, especially when he got the NASA secondment, but he never had a moment like that again. He'd peaked early, like a mathematician.

'Satellite security,' I say. 'What does that even mean? Like, spy satellites?'

'Yes. Technology protecting satellites from attack.'

At the other end of the park, the heli circles and then lands.

'Oh no,' Terry says. 'They've found my device.'

I'M ON MY FEET and pacing, ready to move. The heli is back in the air, getting closer and closer. If we hand Terry over, would they leave us be? Terry looks at me, face sad and puffy, as if I've spoken out loud. Maybe if things had been different, if I'd been born at a different time, I could have been a better person.

May is constructing a world of her own in the dirt with gumnuts, sticks and callitris cones. There are fences, houses and a shared garden plot. Her pigtails flick from side to side as she works.

The meeting is still going. We're far enough away that we can't quite hear what is being said. Which is their intention, but hand gestures, facial expressions and the intensity of the whole thing tell a story. I can almost lipread. Especially my mother and Uncle Nate, whose speech patterns I know. Blair, too. He's kind of predictable in his sentences, the meaning all coming in a rush towards the end. No one shouts or loses their temper; they don't work that way. But it doesn't look like agreement.

At last Des stands and squares his shoulders. He's so easy in his body but there is fierceness there that's a kind of truth. When he speaks, everyone listens.

'This is our moment. The only one we're going to get,' he says.

There is a vote. Everyone raises a hand except for Fran, who is staring at her feet. The circle stills as the decision settles. I can almost feel Earth's rotation, shifting forward, the pull of gravity.

Everyone stands, taking turns to hug Fran. They're wiping their eyes, even Dianella. Then they scramble. It's time to pack up.

Dianella is heading towards us and I don't like the expression on her face. I don't like it at all.

'Okay,' she says. 'May, you need to get ready, sweetie.'

May destroys her world in the dirt with a few hand movements, leaps to her feet and runs to Fran.

Dianella turns to face me. 'Nate will take Fran and May to a safehouse. We'll camp here tonight. And, as soon as Nate returns, we're going back to the observatory.'

'You've got to be kidding,' I say.

'We have to try. If we can commandeer the main telescope, we're still in business,' she says.

'Which business is that?'

'What we need *you* to do is get Terry out of here.'

'Me?!'

Terry looks away and my mother presses her lips together in that particular thin line of disappointment.

'It isn't safe for Terry here,' she says. 'You have three tasks.'

Dianella places an envelope in my hands. I trace the shape of a memory card case with my fingers.

'First, get this into a postbox. The world needs to know what's happening.'

The address is one of Dad's school friends, editor of an independent online journal. 'Will he even be able to read this thing?'

'This is a man who still has a Beta video player, just in case.'

I shake my head. She's talking in riddles again.

'And we need you up on Kaputar, for the total eclipse. When you're in the eye of it, we need you to signal with the laser light. From in front of the radio tower, if you can.'

'But. That's the day after tomorrow.'

She nods. 'You'll need to be in position beforehand. Like for a shoot,' she says. 'It's hard to think while it's happening.'

I've read about total eclipses, people screaming and crying and carrying on. 'I won't get emotional,' I say.

Dianella almost smiles. 'You will, Fin. Everyone does.'

For a second I think my mother is going to hug me but instead, she holds out the black box she thinks she has kept secret from me since we packed our lives into bags.

'This is the third thing.'

'No,' I say. 'I won't take it.' It's not the weight that bothers me, but the responsibility.

'I need you to leave it somewhere safe. Just in case.'

'Is this a suicide mission?'

Dianella sighs. 'It's dangerous. Too dangerous for me to take you.'

'But Jade and Pete are going?'

'Jade was going to go with you. But Terry is here now. And we're going to need Jade's help.'

Terry shuffles further away and scuffs his shoes in the dirt, as if my emotions are a discomfort.

Dianella looks off into the trees, where a robin is calling, and when she speaks again, her voice is soft. 'Remember the Forest Tower, when we camped?'

I nod, sniffing back tears. She knows it's not something I'll forget.

The rails were cold, too cold to touch, the scaffolding shaking in the wind. When we reached the top, Dad lifted me up onto his shoulders. There was nothing but forest in every direction, as far as I could see. As far as Dad's binoculars and Dianella's most powerful telephoto lens could see. The Warrumbungles bordered the Pilliga Forest on one side, the Nandewar Range on the other. Beneath us, the Great Artesian Basin, the largest body of freshwater in the world, shifting like an animal in discomfort. And above us, the full extent of the Milky Way, that river in the sky.

It was the moment when I understood our world. The story of who I am and where we live, the connective tissue holding everything together. All the stories. I just didn't know how fragile it was.

Dianella grips my bicep. 'Remember the plan we made then?'

'Yes.'

'Well, that's what I need you to do now.'

'But how?'

'You'll figure it out. Remember your training. And Terry can help.'

I huff under my breath.

'He will. You'll see.' She hands me a bright orange watch I've never seen before. Digital but old-school. 'I've synchronised this to mine.'

The big black numbers are already moving, counting down. Forty-six hours until the eclipse.

This time my mother does hug me. 'I love you,' she says. 'When I see your signal, I'll know you're safe.'

Fran brings May over to say goodbye. She buries her face in my belly and I hold her to me.

'Hey,' I say. 'Hot shower tonight, huh? Jealous.'

May nods but cannot speak.

'Good luck,' I say.

'You, too,' Fran says. 'Take care.' She reaches for May's hand and leads her away.

The heli is close now, blurring my thoughts.

Uncle Nate has been waiting, eyes skyward. He hands Terry a small backpack. 'We've put together some kit for you. Sleeping bag, thermarest, tent, clean clothes, fleece, extra food, water bottle. And some of those bars you like, Finley.'

Terry takes the pack and hugs it to their chest. 'Thank you.'

Uncle Nate turns to me and smiles. 'Told you I'd see you soon.'

'And now you're going,' I say.

'Everyone's going,' Uncle Nate says. 'To put an end to all of this. For good.'

Everyone except me. 'I can't walk to Kaputar in two days. Not with Terry.'

'I'd take one of the old Parks vehicles, I reckon.'

I laugh. 'Of course.' Why didn't I think of that?

He puts his hands on my shoulders. 'Remember. You're never alone out there, okay?'

CIVIL TWILIGHT

Warrumbungle National Park

Gamilaraay Country

45:30:00

TERRY'S GRIPLESS STREET SHOES slip and slide on the gravel slope. I focus on the chatter of thornbills, the wattles already dressed in yellow. The sun is dropping fast. There is no way I can make it to the Parks depot before dark with Terry slowing me down. We'll have to camp somewhere and get away early in the morning.

The track flattens out as we approach Split Rock, late light warming the stone. It's another one of those special places. No one particular spot that I've found so far but the whole formation. Spending time there has always accelerated some kind of emotional shift. Like when I decided I wasn't going to date anyone at school again; it wasn't worth the drama.

It would be better to shelter in one of the caves up on Split Rock, overlooking the valley and the observatory, but there is too much risk of being seen.

Dianella loved to photograph the galactic core erupting from the gap between Split Rock's twin peaks, tapping into some old volcanic alchemy. When Hild came with us one night, she suggested that it looked more like a bodily eruption, which set her and Dianella giggling while I rolled my eyes. Hild kind of got my mother, and Dianella loved Hild. No one else was welcome on weekends, let alone on astro expeditions. And for me, being around Dianella was easier with Hild there.

That last time we went out the skies clouded over, so we packed up and sat around the campfire instead, sipping the butterscotch schnapps Hild had brought along. Again, not something I could have got away with. The flames mirrored the heat of the liquid flickering inside me.

Hild leaned forward, her face serious. 'How do you keep going, Nell?'

'Are you asking me if I have hope?' Dianella said.

'No,' Hild said. 'We …' She glanced at me. 'We think hope is self-indulgent.'

I closed my eyes. Although Hild and I often talked this way when alone, it wasn't a topic I would have dared raise with my mother. It was a hole I didn't want to fall into.

Dianella nodded. 'Can you explain?'

'Hope isn't something we can afford. It's like people just want to hear that they don't have to change the way they're living.'

'My generation, you mean?'

The flames had subsided into coals, a deep red glow. Hild's face was half in shadow. 'We want to know what we can *do*.'

Dianella smiled. 'You girls are going to be just fine,' she said. 'Hope comes from doing. My photography has always been my centre. I'm lucky that it dovetails with my activism. You'll find your own way to action,' she said. 'And stick together. I'd be lost without Phil. It's too much to carry on your own.'

45:15:00

I LEAD US AWAY from the main trail, northwest, towards Burbie Canyon. The path narrows as it shifts to follow the creek. Frogs call to one another, warning of our passing. Was it only this morning that I woke with pobblebonks? A family of goats crash off into the undergrowth, leaving behind their sharp stink. When humans are long gone, there will be goats, crows and ticks. I don't follow the thought too far; at least one of the meals we're carrying will be goat-based.

I stop short of the road and listen for oncoming vehicles, footsteps or voices but after all the action of the day, the park is quiet.

'We'll cross here,' I say. 'Quick.'

I sprint across the pitted bitumen, checking every direction with all my senses, like a shield, and stopping only when I reach the cover of the trees. Terry hesitates before moving and their movements are awkward, but they make it. Behind those thick glasses, their eyes are red.

A wallaby track takes us down to Wambelong Creek, its banks torn into a bog by goats and pigs. We follow the water, treetops reflected in its slow-moving surface, until it intersects with the trail we need to take. I cross on a string of stones and wait for Terry.

Our progress is quicker on the paved track, flat and wide. Thick black clouds streak across a rose sky in weird spectral shapes. Rain is coming. The track steepens, weaving through a sea of yellow everlasting daisies. The light is leaving, and Terry is fading fast.

'There's a cave just up here,' I say.

Terry glances at me but says nothing. I don't like caves much either. They're cold and damp. But it's better than getting rained on and carrying heavy wet gear tomorrow. It was open to tourists once, and the Gamilaraay have used it for generations, so it can't be too bad. I just hope there isn't anyone living in it.

The timber boardwalk lifts us above the dense black wattle regrowth, from the last wave of fires. I turn to look back over the park, to Belougery, far away now, in golden hour. For a moment, I feel the pinch of distance from my mother. Are my tasks really part of their plans, or just a convenient way of getting rid of us? Terry was bringing the heat on them, and I was in the way.

Terry runs into the back of me, knocking me off balance. I open my mouth to swear. But it's me who has stopped in the middle of the path and lost focus. On the boardwalk, Terry can almost keep up.

I feel the change in texture on my skin when we reach the sandstone slopes, and the subtle shift in smell. The presence of other beings all around, their awareness of us and the disturbance we bring.

◠

We're into civil twilight before we reach the protective scaffolding around the cave. I stop short of the entrance and listen for human noise but there is only the scuffling of small animals, and the wingbeat of an owl nearby.

'Hey,' I say. 'I'm Fin Kelvin. From down south, Ngunnawal Country, but I live here now, in the park. We seek shelter from the rain that's coming and those that hunt us. We won't stop long.' There is no response, no sign either way that I can pick up, though I feel the cool change that has moved through on my cheeks. I wish I hadn't used the word 'hunted'. They are hunting Terry. Me, too, but now I can't help but think of older violence, and caves as places of last refuge. The land holds memories and some of those memories are heavy. Terry rubs the skin on their forearms as if everything hurts.

I remove my pack and stand in the mouth of the cave until my eyes adjust. The lock has been forced and the gate dragged open. The stone slab with its deep grinding grooves has been exposed but seems unharmed. Dry wallaby droppings and fresh lizard tracks mark the dust. The air is cool and not too stale, though it reeks of bat shit. I find a flat spot and lay out my swag. Terry drops the bag a respectful distance away and stands arms by their sides, looking around. I set up my bed and stretch myself out on the ground, head on my pack, trying to make sense of the day.

Terry is still standing there, clicking their fingers. Some sort of weird nervous tic. They move towards the back of the cave, where I have zero interest in going. The clicking is faster now, echoing around the cave, reverberating in my inner ear. Bats shuffle and chirrup from somewhere high up.

'Can you stop that?'

'I want to know what's in here,' Terry says. They're leaning forward, into the darkness.

I rummage in the pocket of my pack for my headtorch. But when I hold it out, I see that Terry's eyes are closed.

'You can echolocate.'

'Yes.'

'From birth?'

'Before I had glasses, I couldn't see far. It was just something I did.'

'Is it really seeing with sound?'

'For me it's more like touching. The response to the sounds,' Terry says. 'I can feel the density and texture. Stone and glass are bright, and dirt and leaves are dark. It comes in flashes.'

'This is why they want to study you?'

Terry hesitates before nodding.

'I'm sorry.'

'It isn't your fault,' Terry says.

'Can ... others do this?'

'Some.'

Before the Incompletes, there were a handful of people with the ability to navigate through echolocation. But they were born blind. Our brains can adapt, develop senses humans had forgotten. Those people, too, were studied and written about. They were known by number only, their identities protected, to avoid being hounded for studies and interviews.

Terry walks back to the exact spot where they dropped the bag, unclips it and extracts the sleeping bag and thermarest by feel. Only then, after I have seen what they can do, do I turn on my headtorch.

'Are you hungry?'

'Not really. Too tired,' Terry says.

'Me either,' I say. And I can't be bothered cooking. 'But drink lots of water, okay?'

Terry nods, already unscrewing the lid of the bottle.

I wash my hands, face and feet, strip down to T-shirt and undies, and am burrowing into my sleeping bag when I hear them. Drones. A line of drones combing the park. I switch off my headtorch.

Terry sits up.

'They shouldn't be able to get a read in here,' I say. 'But hold the base of the sleeppad up between you and the cave mouth. Make sure your sleeping bag is zipped up and your hood pulled in tight around your face. Stay as still as you can.'

'Thermal imaging?' Terry says.

'Yep.'

They sent the drones out after us one night, not long after we left the observatory. We were lucky. It was winter and everyone was already in bed. Our sleeping bags limited the heat read. Most of us had survival blankets over us, too, which must have broken up our thermal signature. And maybe government drones aren't the best. After that we carried those blankets everywhere, until Blair stayed up all night attaching a special coating to the base of everyone's mattresses.

The high, whining buzz moves closer and closer, until the line reaches us. A single drone hovers at the entrance to the cave. I hold my breath, hoping we are deep enough in, the cave mouth too narrow. The noise, the vibration, the threat they carry, makes it hard to think.

Within its noise, I can sense the whir of the camera lens, straining to see. *I hate drones.* And then it's gone, with a rising whine, speeding off to rejoin the line. My thoughts fly to my mother, Jade, Des and Blair, out in the open. Uncle Nate on his way back from the safehouse. I can only hope that they hear them coming.

Terry's breaths are short and shallow.

'We're okay,' I say. 'Try to get some rest.'

37:11:00

IT'S STILL ASTRONOMICAL DARK when I step outside the cave. Terry has stopped crying at last but I've given up trying to sleep. A powerful owl calls down in the valley and is answered from far away. The rain has cleared the air, giving me the best view of the stars I've had for months.

'Hey, Betel,' I say. 'We have to leave, and I don't want to.'

He doesn't really answer but he'll be there, wherever I go.

Venus is up, diamond white, the only female planet. I can make out the bright smudges of the Magellanic Clouds, the dwarf galaxies named for the sixteenth-century Portuguese explorer, even though the Persian astronomer, Sufi, wrote about them centuries earlier. And they were named and storied for tens of thousands of years before that, by First Peoples.

Now a committee governs the naming system. Planets are all named after Roman and Greek gods, and their moons and features have a theme relating to that god. Mars was the Roman god of war, who the Greeks called Ares. So Mars' moons are named after Ares' sons, Phobos and Deimos, who drove his chariot into battle. They're not even really moons, just two lumpy asteroids trapped in Mars' orbit. Phobos means fear and panic and Deimos means terror and dread, which pretty much set the tone for the exploration of space.

Those names were suggested by a science master at Eton College two centuries ago, taking them from the *Iliad*. Dad called books like that classics. Dianella calls it an epic white male fantasy, and Eton the last bastion of the middle ages. She says that what separates men from women – like life is still so binary – is that men today still fantasise about the Roman Empire. 'And we all know what happened there.'

If I don't look directly at him, I can see Antares, the other red star in Scorpius, literally named 'not Ares'. He has already consumed all his hydrogen. One day he'll go supernova, like Betel. By then Betel will be gone. He's probably already gone. And I'm talking to no one.

'Light is so slow to arrive,' Dad said. 'When we look at the stars, we're actually looking into the past. And the farther away we're looking, the further back in time we're seeing. We see the sun as it looked eight minutes ago, and Sirius the way it appeared in the seventeenth century. We can't even be sure that anything we're looking at is still there.'

We were standing outside the lodge in the dark. The magnitude of time and space and the smallness of me was overwhelming. Dad wrapped one arm around my shoulders and the other around my mother's waist.

Dianella, who saw the same sky through different lenses, smiled in the dark. 'But the stars are our future, too.'

The idea settled me somehow. My mother was more optimistic then. She had Dad, and I had both of them.

Dad's NASA secondment was part of the Artemis campaign, advising on the Road to Mars project. He spent most of the time in a lab, poring over data and images, he said, while they completed the first stage: turning the moon into a refuelling station. He ran a side project, analysing the composition of moon rock, and comparing it to the origin stars, trying to put together a timeline for Earth and the universe.

Moon rock had a smell at first, he said. Though it faded later. And the dust, when he broke rocks apart, got everywhere, making his eyes water and his nose run.

Dianella said she started making him shower as soon as he got back to the apartment provided for them, worried that moon dust would get into her camera equipment.

Her lab was on the other side of the NASA centre, as part of a team working to produce higher quality imagery from the space telescopes. It's hard to imagine now, but Dianella started out taking photos through telescopes. Lens upon lens between her and the stars. Her early images were of the insides of the Magellanic Clouds and the luminous gases and star clusters of the Tarantula Nebula. It was a kind of fantasy world, launched into the public imagination.

Once she met Uncle Nate and Des and learned about cultural astronomy, its history, and the threats to its future, she left the telescopes to Dad.

Even if he never made the headlines again, Dad made everyone's lives bigger. He mapped stellar streams, the filaments of stars orbiting the edges of our galaxy, and found remnants of dwarf galaxies that had been absorbed into our own. His work showed that the Milky Way grows by dragging in and consuming smaller stellar streams. The Milky Way is getting fatter, like other peoples' parents.

Those stellar streams also allowed Dad's team to better understand the properties of dark matter, the particles that don't absorb, reflect, or emit light, and yet hold the universe together. It's all around us, everywhere, holding us together, too. I can't touch or see it, but it's dark matter that allows me to sense the world the way I do. If that isn't magic, what is?

The old Greek and Roman naming conventions don't apply to stellar streams. One of them is called Wambelong, after our creek, here in the park.

35:12:00

AFTER THE STARS HAVE faded and the first hint of light appears in the east, I return to the cave.

'It's morning, Terry,' I say. 'We need to go.'

Terry struggles out of the sleeping bag, still fully clothed, and reaches for their glasses. I pack up my gear while Terry goes outside to pee, then boil water for tea. I wait for it to brew, squeeze a big dollop of sweetened condensed milk into both mugs, stir them, and set one down next to Terry.

'Thank you.'

I sit at the entrance, nursing my tea and chewing an oat bar, watching Terry struggle to stuff the sleeping bag back into its sack.

'Do you prefer they or he?'

'He, I think.' Terry shrugs. 'You?'

'Fin,' I say. 'Or she, I think.'

The corner of his mouth shifts. 'Okay.' He gulps down a mouthful of tea, and then another. I rinse my cup, pack up the cooker, and stow them in my pack.

Terry slurps some more and hands me his cup. 'Ready.'

I toss out the rest of the tea, slip the cup in the side pocket of my pack, hand him an oat bar and start walking.

There is just enough light to follow the path back down the hill towards Wambelong Creek without torches. Terry is close behind me, close enough that I hear him chewing and breathing. It's annoying – but not as annoying as yesterday, somehow. And me being annoyed doesn't help him get any better at things.

I indicate the firetrail with my left hand and we follow it. I'd like to run, but can walk nearly as fast and, for now, Terry is keeping up.

I turn and try for a smile. 'You're doing great.'

The firetrail loops around to the big campgrounds. It's the long way but the safer way, far from the road and the observatory and whatever is going on there. A yellow robin *tchew tchews* close by, hidden in the gloom. Kookaburras telegraph from far away. The sun is up but yet to reach us. Creatures shift and stir above and below ground, in the pause before another day rushes us forwards again.

My parents didn't meet online like normal people, but at a One Sky conference. They were on some panel together and Dad made the mistake of suggesting that astrophotography was tricked-up, over-processed and the colours exaggerated.

My mother took the bait. 'Have you seen NASA's photographs? It's like someone spilled the food dye,' she said.

That got a laugh from the audience.

'I only show what's already there,' she said.

The way my mother tells the story, no one had ever stood up to Professor Kelvin before. Dad looked at the giant screen behind them, displaying her image of an aqua plasma arc near the Andromeda Galaxy. 'Your pictures *are* very beautiful,' he said. 'And you're right. We're all here to help people see.'

My mother was beautiful, too. She wore her hair short then, accentuating her strong jaw, and a long dress smoothed her edges. He found my mother at drinks afterwards and asked all about her process. She sent him back to the hotel bar to fetch a second glass of champagne before she thawed enough to ask him a single question. But it was a big one: why astronomy?

'It was the expression on his face when he spoke,' she says. 'His ideas were so expansive. And it did help that he was handsome.'

They shared a sense of wonder at the night sky, outer space, that great unknown. And after that, they were always on the same side, though they didn't always agree on the method.

⸻

I slow as we approach the edge of the main campground. Dad and I used to walk early mornings, among the old trees, to see musk lorikeets and red-rumped parrots. Dianella and I arrived in the evenings, when the moon was dark, to capture the Milky Way suspended over the range.

A whiff of human occupation intrudes: food, urine, wool, and sunscreen. I hold up my arm. Terry bumps into the back of my pack and winds himself.

'Shh,' I say.

But the campground is deserted. Just a flattened square of grass where a tent has been pitched and two damp patches nearby. If they hadn't already moved on before the helis, they have now.

I let out the breath I've been holding and lead us to the creek. Tiny bubbles stream to the surface, like filaments of light. We follow the water, trying not to splash, until we hit the walking trail that leads to the Discovery Centre. A swamp wallaby stares for a moment before thumping away.

Across the paddocks, the sun hits the white dome of the main telescope. For so long it has been the beacon of the park, and the park my playground. But now there are vehicles, helis, and soldiers planning their next moves. It's no longer a safe place. It is no longer mine.

30:45:00

WE CROUCH IN THE cover of trees, just short of the old Parks depot. I half-expect it to be occupied, too. But it's empty and quiet. I snip through the links of the fence with Dad's multi-tool, peeling back the netting to create a hole just big enough for us to crawl through. Terry follows me in, dragging the packs. From the mess of tools, vehicles, signs and gear, staff must have left in a hurry.

The electric vehicles – white four-wheel drives and utes – are all flat, and we don't have time to charge a battery. When I try the ignition of one of the new all-terrain vehicles, it's flat, too. I head for the older-model ATVs instead, up the back. The largest of them, a late hybrid, looks most promising. When I turn on the ignition, the gauge says full but I don't know if the fuel will be any good, how long it has been sitting in the tank. The more immediate problem is that the ATV is parked in by other vehicles. And the sun is up. It's only a matter of time until that heli starts searching again.

The electric vehicles, without power, without gears, cannot be moved. The mower will be easiest to shift. I release the handbrake and slip it into neutral.

'Help me push,' I say.

There isn't much of Terry, but he puts everything into it. Together we jam the mower hard up against the vehicle in front, giving us just enough room to get out our ATV.

At first it doesn't even turn over but on the third try, the engine coughs. And on the fourth, it starts. I leave it running while I fill two empty fuel canisters from the depot tank, hoping that the larger body of fuel will be in better condition. The stink of diesel burns my nostrils, and some splashes on my hands as I finish. I slip the containers into the racks at the front of the vehicle.

I wash my hands at the sink and dry them on an old towel. The key hanging on a hook is labelled GATE, which I take. There is all manner of camping gear, an unopened box of powerbars, a row of hiking boots on timber shelves and, beneath them, piles of uniforms: shirts, pants and hats. I fill my pockets with powerbars, grab two shirts, two pairs of pants, two beanies, a pair of boots closest to Terry's sneaker size, and a billy, and throw it all on the passenger-side floor.

I feel the vibration in my inner ear before I hear it. The heli warming up.

Terry is still standing there. 'Will I put our bags in the back?'

'Yeah. And quick.' I climb into the driver's seat and throw the helmets out onto the ground. 'C'mon.'

Terry hesitates, taking in the vehicle without doors or seatbelts, without screens or audio instructions. His face does have expressions; they're just harder to read.

I put my foot on the accelerator, harder than is necessary, before Terry is quite settled in the passenger seat. There is no point asking him to open the gates, so I get out myself, release the lock and swing them outwards. Then I run back to the ATV, jump in and zoom through, gunning it as we hit the gravel. The wheels skid and slide.

When we reach the main road, I head east, though it will take us back past the observatory. It's the quickest way to the Pilliga. The tyres grip the tar and I put my foot to the floor. The engine is loud. Too loud.

Top speed is only about seventy-five kilometres an hour. It's a lot quicker than we could walk but not enough to outrun another vehicle. And certainly not a heli.

'Is it in the air?'

Terry turns in his seat. 'Not yet.'

The air is cold, stinging my face. I don't know if or when I'll be back. I allow myself a moment to watch the light on Belougery Spire and then the thin volcanic dyke once known as the Breadknife. The mountains who have been my backbone. Then the road dips and rises, swinging around, hiding the range from view. The tears that come dry before they reach my cheeks.

Terry watches the road behind us. The bitumen is rough, pitted and patched, whole sections washed out. Heavy vehicle traffic has crumbled the edges. I stick to the middle, the white centreline disappearing beneath us, as if I own the road.

'It's up,' Terry says.

'What's it doing?' We have to lean towards each other and yell to be heard over the engine.

'Circling around and ... going the other way. Fast.'

'We're sitting ducks if they look back.'

But the heli keeps going. In a straight line, as if they know where they're headed.

Terry turns, as if he's had the same thought. *The others.*

'They'll hear it,' I say.

Terry nods and blows out his cheeks.

I'm tense as we approach the turnoff to the observatory, watching for vehicles snaking down through forest. But it comes from the other side of the road: a beat-up white van with solar panels covering its roof creeps out from the cluster of buildings at the base of the hill. The van flies out without checking left or right. There are silhouettes in all the windows. They're heading out of the park, towards town. I lift my foot from the accelerator until the van moves away, out of sight. If anyone does turn around, it doesn't slow their pace.

Maybe it's the lack of doors and windows, the noise and cold and wind tearing at us, but our vulnerability hits me. Me, an Illegal, and Terry's face, in this ridiculous vehicle. We have no idea what we're heading into.

29:10:00

THE FIRST TWINGES OF period pain tug at my lower belly. It's early, by two days at least, but unmistakeable. I grope under the seat for the first-aid kit, hoping to find some ibuprofen, but the shelf is broken, and empty. *Idiot.* That was the first thing I should have checked. And raided the other vehicles for their kits.

We pass empty farmhouses, tiny homes and dongas crowded onto bare blocks, makeshift banks of solar panels, car and van bodies, and a string of mailboxes sculpted from recycled scrap: wombats, echidnas, a wedge-tailed eagle. Dust swirls in dry yard after dry yard.

A dark four-wheel drive approaches from the other direction. Terry turns away. I lift two fingers from the steering wheel as they pass, the way the rangers used to. The driver stares. I think he's going to stop and turn around but he continues on his way.

When we pass the rusty life-size emu sculpture that I used to look out for, I slow down. The faded red postbox is still on the corner of the laneway. I pull over in a spray of gravel and take the envelope Dianella has entrusted to me from my shirt pocket. The pictures won't tell the full story. But maybe they tell something. I leap out and slip the package into the slot. Only once I've let go, and hear the envelope hit the bottom, do I question whether the box is still emptied. The notice setting out collection days and times is faded beyond legibility. Surely the box would have been removed if it was no longer in service. Wouldn't it?

Pointless task number one: tick. I make the shape in the air with my finger and walk back to the ATV.

Terry takes the little bottle from his pocket, removes his glasses and tucks them in his shirt pocket. He opens the bottle, tips his head back and squeezes a single drop in each eye.

'They get dry?'

He blinks, long eyelashes fluttering. When he puts his glasses back on, his pupils are enlarged, his irises violet.

'Whoa,' I say.

'They do get dry. But the drops are for myopia. Atropine. It slows the elongation of my eyeballs. My glasses do, too. The lenses tweak the light, trick my brain.'

'Slows, not stops?'

'Yes. But slowing the progression reduces the impact by half.'

'How long do you have to use them?'

'Until I stop growing,' he says.

I can't think that far ahead. 'Let's put this gear on,' I say. 'Maybe we can pass as Parks staff.'

Terry looks around, for cover, I'm guessing. I just turn my back and change beside the vehicle. I can feel Terry's embarrassment in the silence. But when I turn around, he's wearing the shirt, which fits, and the pants, which are a little long but can be rolled up. We put on the fleeces and the beanies, making sure the Parks insignia is above our faces.

Terry sits in the passenger seat to try on the boots, bracing one foot at a time against the glovebox, to tighten the laces. He struggles to tie them off but eventually gets there.

'Comfortable?'

He turns his feet in a circle and paddles them up and down against the floor. 'Yes.'

'Is there a first-aid kit in there?' I gesture to the glovebox.

Terry pushes on the button with one finger and the cover drops open. Bingo. Binoculars, goggles and a small but newish first-aid kit.

'Can you see if there are any painkillers in that green bag with a cross?'

Terry examines the labels on each of the packets.

'Yep, that one,' I say.

I pop out two capsules wash them down with a mouthful of water.

Terry rummages in the glovebox. and pulls out a rectangular plastic device.

'What is this?'

'An old voice recorder, maybe. A dictaphone.' That was one of Dad's words.

Terry presses the largest button. A female voice speaks, wavering, as if it has been stretched thin. 'So. This is it. The last day. Tomorrow the park is closing, my job is ending. Or they're going to stop paying me, anyway. We're going to stay. I'm worried about all the birds and animals who've been sheltering here. I'm worried about Ilse. She says her life is over. Our life. It isn't fair on any of us. But I guess fair or right doesn't come into it ...'

'Turn that off,' I say.

Terry peers at the buttons and presses something that stops Gina's voice.

I start the ATV and pull back onto the road. The white lines blur.

Gina was our senior ranger and Ilse was one of our field officers. The day they closed the park, all the activists and podcasters came, from as far away as Brisbane. We knew they were coming; we'd tipped them off, to expose the injustice.

What we didn't know was that with them all assembled in front of the stone entrance, holding out their cameras and devices, Ilse would douse herself in fuel and light a match. Gina was right there but couldn't stop her. We were all there. Dad pulled me into his body, to try to stop me seeing – but I had seen enough to imagine the rest. And he couldn't block her screams. Or the smell. I'll never forget that smell. The images reached the screens of millions, were replayed thousands of times, but changed nothing.

And Gina, in those moments afterwards, lost control. All that anger and pain and ... When she was arrested, Blair and

Dianella went to the station and engaged a solicitor, but we never saw Gina again.

I push down hard on the accelerator, shifting my weight into the curves. There are moments, moments like this, where it could break you. When the past bubbles up, swallowing hope, swallowing the future. Dad taught me to breathe through it, to focus on something specific and beautiful. Like the deep blue-green of a rockpool as you dive in, and the shock of cold on your skin.

After a couple of tries picturing the water below Horton Falls, with a lot of breathing, it works. The bitumen comes back into focus, the double white line. Terry is still sitting there, looking at me with those strange eyes, his wide forehead pinched.

'Are you okay?'

I nod. Knowing that I can come out the other side, having done it once and now a hundred times, I know I can get through anything.

28:40:00

WE PASS A TATTERED camp next to the mottled mound that is the town tip. Bits of paper and an empty plastic bottle blow about in circles. The striped caravan awnings are faded and some of the lean-to structures have collapsed, as if it has been cleared out or abandoned. There are more cars on the road as we pass the medium-density resettlements, all dark roofs and high fences. Bright digital signs promise a better life through rural community living.

'Did you come in this way?'

'No,' Terry says. 'Up the highway, past Dubbo.'

Two new electric sedans overtake us, heading into Coonabarabran. 'That's close enough to town, I think.'

I turn off onto a treelined stockroute heading northwest. A few big old mother trees are hanging on, a litter of fallen limbs beneath them. Some of the hollows might still harbour a galah or rosella but it's mostly crows we see, with their giant beaks and eyes, searching for food.

I turn onto a backroad, then another stockroute, working my way north.

'Do you even know where you're going?' Terry says.

'Yep,' I say.

I know the park and its surrounds from maps, apps and family excursions. We walked every corner of the Warrumbungles. Some walks required leaving the park and re-entering it. Or it was easier to drive to the trailhead than bush-bash over mountains. My parents had friends in the area who we used to visit, too. Like the Chapmans, with their alpaca farm, and the Needhams, who inherited an old forty-inch telescope and built a shed around it.

'Are there blank tapes for that recorder?' I say.

Terry rummages in the glovebox and holds up the packet. There is only one missing, the one in the machine. The other five are still wrapped tight in plastic.

I give Terry a thumbs-up.

He rearranges the glovebox and shuts it. 'How long to go?'

'Forest Tower this afternoon.'

'And after that?'

'Kaputar tomorrow morning. If everything goes smoothly,' I say.

Terry tips his head to check my watch and mouths the word *smoothly*. A comment on the road, perhaps, which is ridged and full of potholes.

'Did you get teased at school?' I say.

'My parents home-schooled me.'

'Mine, too. Year eleven and twelve anyway.'

Terry keeps his eyes on the road ahead. 'I learn better that way. But ... I know I'm not so good with people.'

❦

My parents made sure my formal education continued. Dad taught me maths, physics – and astronomy, of course. Dianella tried to teach me English and history but neither of us could sit still with books for long. We agreed it was a waste of time trying to follow the curriculum if I couldn't sit the exams. We read novels or watched a film together instead, and discussed them afterwards.

The park had already taught me natural history and geology. Millions of years ago, the Warrumbungles was a massive shield volcano. The land was restless, still having its pyroclastic eruptions. Molten lava pushed its way up through cracks in the sandstone to reach the surface in thick plugs, cooling into trachyte. The shield is long gone, eroded away by the elements. Only the plugs, dykes, cones, and pillars remain. It's a lesson in deep time. But when I close my eyes, I can't picture our ridgeline as well as I could. As if that landscape has already started releasing me.

I did a term with Uncle Nate out on the trails, helping with cultural burns, track clearing, planting, weeding and seed collection. That's when he said I could call him uncle. Then my parents got fixated on problem-solving as a self-sufficiency tool. For the world I was inheriting, Dianella said.

The problems Dad set for me were usually indoors and intellectual. Like leaving me a note in code, which I had to crack without any clues. He taught me some tricks, like looking for single-letter words, which can only be I or A. And that *the* and *and* are the most common three-letter words, with E and T the most-used letters. I liked to check for double letters, too. Dad cheated, in that he didn't use apostrophes, which would have made it easier. Sometimes he made up the code or used a passage from a book. Sometimes it was an actual code from history, which would be followed by a history lesson, usually about war. I argued that if I cracked the code, I should skip the lesson, as a reward, but he said that was never going to fly.

Dianella's lessons were variations on endurance and torture. Tasks that appeared straightforward but when I reached what I thought was the destination or prize, like using a map and compass to find a food cache, there would just be a key and another set of coordinates that took me even further from home. There, I'd find a lockbox, which would contain, at last, food and drink. I started packing my own provisions as the expeditions got longer and longer. Maybe that was all I was supposed to learn.

There were no allowances made for bad weather or period pain. One time I ended up lost on Wedding Cake Mountain as a storm swept in, and stumbled into a cave to wait it out. When I turned on my headtorch, I saw that it was a Gamilaraay gallery, full of hand stencils and animals and star maps. I haven't told a soul. Or asked Uncle Nate if he knew it, though I wanted to. I should never have been there.

Dianella seemed almost disappointed when I turned up back at the house, dry and cheerful.

27:50:00

I SQUAT BEHIND THE ATV to pee. When I wipe myself, the tissue comes away red. I fold the square, drop it in our rubbish bag, and wash my hands. When I check my toiletries kit, my cup isn't in there. I must have left it on the shelf in the shower back at the cabin. I fish around in the first-aid kit for tampons. There are only two.

A mob of apostlebirds land, hopping over the ground around the ATV in search of scraps. They're real characters, strutting around in grey and brown, with dark frowning eyes and scolding chatter, but they've become such scavengers. I lunge at them, and they fly up onto a branch, arranging themselves in a line to stare down on me in judgement.

We've seen no other wildlife in the air or on the ground. The cattle in the bare paddock on the other side of the fence are Herefords, with white faces and red bodies, which you don't see much anymore. There are no calves among them. A steer strains at the wires to reach a tuft of grass on the other side.

I take the recorder from the glovebox, remove the tape and place it back in its little case. An old felt-tip marker works well enough to label it. I place a fresh tape in the machine and clear my throat. But where does this story start exactly? When the first Incomplete was born, when the Great Thinning began, or right back at the arrival of those white ships?

'I was just a little kid when we made the Forest Tower plan. If there was a natural disaster, or the world was ending in any of the ways we thought it could, and if we were separated for some reason, we would meet up there. And if any of us had to move on, we would leave a message saying where we were going. My idea – a child's idea – was that we should leave a message for the world, or whoever came after, explaining what had happened. And maybe then, it wouldn't happen again, the way it seemed to happen over and over to human civilisations. But I never imagined that I would actually have to do it. Especially not alone.'

Terry reappears from behind a clump of dying stringybarks, stumbling over the furrows and squeezing back through the fence. For whatever reason, he needs to go a long way away from me to pee.

I stop the machine and put it back in the glovebox.

'Are you leaving a voicey?' Terry says.

'Something like that,' I say.

I hand Terry the sanitiser. 'Where were you going to go, in Queensland?'

'To an island,' Terry says. 'We had to change cars at the edge of the national park and again at the border. And then take a ferry. A colleague of Dad's has a house over there.'

'I've never even been to Queensland,' I say.

'It's very hot, apparently. But the island looked nice. There are still some turtles, Mum said.'

Terry has that look, like he might cry. They would have been there by now. Happy and safe – for a while. I don't even know what to suggest about finding his parents. Or what will happen after the eclipse. Instead, I imagine walking through a ribbon of rainforest, out to the white sand, into that warm blue water, to swim with turtles. Their undersides are pale and smooth, their swimming strokes graceful despite their great shells.

26:05:00

I MAKE ONLY ONE wrong turn, but it takes me fifteen minutes to realise. The shortcut back to the road crosses private property. I drop the pace to reduce noise, and the plume of dust behind us. Heat shimmers over bare paddocks. We cross a cattle grid, shaking everything loose in the ATV and juddering our whole bodies.

A green ute crawls across the paddock. The person standing on the back is holding something long and thin that glints in the sun. The driver beeps the horn. Terry sits up straight, body tense. I raise my arm above the frame of the ATV and wave. They don't wave back.

Skinny cattle mill over the road, Angus this time. Terry tucks his hands under his legs as I push through them. Their dark eyes turn towards us and some lean their heads inside the ATV. Terry flattens himself against the seat.

'Do they bite?'

'They're just curious. And used to being fed.'

The ute stops and the person on the back jumps down. It's just a girl with a pitchfork. They're farmers loading hay into long narrow bins. I rev the engine and push forward, into the mob, trusting that the cattle will move.

At last, we're in the clear, bumping over another metal grid, leaving the cattle behind. The road dips into a shallow watercourse. I accelerate out the other side, sending muddy water flying up around us, spraying the windscreen and our faces.

I spot where the track rejoins the road we should have been on and accelerate away, no longer caring about dust or noise. When I take the turn, it's with more confidence than I had when we started out. The ATV isn't so different to the smaller one I used to drive around the park.

The freshly-graded road will take us back to the highway. We've made it. My mistake has only cost us time. But I can't help thinking how easily our luck could run out. That eventually it will. And there is another thought that I've been pushing away: what Dianella and the others are doing, if they're safe. I can no longer see them in my mind.

When we drove Dad to Parkes, Dianella and I stayed near the hospital, in a rental with a rooftop garden overlooking the town. It was just a few dead pot plants arranged around a mat of synthetic grass, but it was her reason for choosing the place. As far as I knew, she spent her nights up there with her cameras, although in that sea of artificial light, visibility must have been poor.

I spent my time in the chair next to Dad's hospital bed, reading *My Side of the Mountain* out loud. The nurses said he could hear me, and it gave me something to do. In some ways, the Catskills are a lot like the Warrumbungles, though we don't have autumn colours or even much of a winter anymore.

From the seventh floor, glassed off from fresh air and sound, with Dad strung up to monitoring machines and plastic bags, I had a fisheye view of the Parkes Precinct. At the crossroads of two major rail lines, goods could be delivered to most of the country within twenty-four hours. The food hub's endless rows of warehouses were lit up like a round-the-clock concert.

The observatory had worked with council and businesses to limit the lighting, providing subsidies to choose dark-sky-friendly globes that could be dimmed through peak galactic visibility periods. Dad used to joke about having the power to turn off whole streets. But transporting goods was deemed more important than discovering the depths of our universe, and Dad's powers were revoked.

The Hospital Precinct came later. It had wings for all the new cancers and a whole floor for lunar silicosis. The moon dust carried back to Earth on rover tyres, high-vis spacesuits, boots, gloves and rock samples clung to everything, especially the inside of human lungs.

One night, Dad woke up and said, 'You'd better fetch Nelly.'

My mother did come then, pacing the room rather than occupying the chair I had vacated for her. She and I looked at each other across the bed, over Dad's wasted body, in that cold green light, and made a decision without speaking. We weren't going to let him die there; it was too terrible.

We waited until changeover, the start of the graveyard shift. It was literal; dozens died every night, just on his floor. The whole of the basement was a morgue, cleared weekly. I'd been roaming that miserable building for weeks, absorbing every pattern: the routes in and out, the emergency exits, the inner clock of the staffing roster. Dianella parked our car right out front, leaving a fake disability permit on the dash. It wasn't the first time I'd seen it. It had made getting a park during school pick-up time a lot easier.

Dianella had form. If you take photographs at night, sooner or later you're going to come to the attention of police. She could justify almost anything for the possibility of capturing a great image. And later, to gather evidence or convey a message.

She stood in the doorway, deactivating the security cameras with her device, while I took Dad's drip from the metal arm and hung it on the bedrail. I dialled down the sound on the monitors and wheeled the bed towards the door until the tubes were stretched tight. My mother came in to remove the cannula, and the beeping started. Not loud, but lights would be flashing somewhere, and someone was meant to be monitoring them.

Dianella pushed the bed from behind, straight out the door, then swung it wide to take the corner, arms straining, the way we used to with shopping trolleys in the Dubbo supermarket. It wasn't fun or funny, the way things used to be, but there was a satisfaction to it. We were *doing* something at last.

I ran to the service lift and held the doors open with my boot while I pulled the bed inside. Dianella squeezed in beside me. I pressed the button for down. The doors closed. Dad's face was serene as we slipped nurses' scrubs on over our thermals and fleece. I didn't ask where Dianella got them.

'We're taking you home, Dad,' I said. 'Back to the park.'

⸺

Terry and I wait in tree shadow, at the edge of the highway, for a break in the traffic. Everyone's eyes are on the road or a screen. It's like Dianella says: most people don't look, and even if they do, they don't see.

We watch a relentless parade of vans, caravans, and camper trailers all heading north. It can only be for the eclipse. There are almost no vehicles going south. Astro-tourism was always big in the park, especially around major cosmic events. And this time, the region will be in the centreline of the moon's shadow, lengthening the totality, which won't happen again for four hundred years. But it feels like more than that, somehow. As if there is more at stake.

'Was there a lot of talk about this eclipse?'

'Yes,' Terry says. 'Christian leaders are saying it is an act of God, a sign. Maybe ... like at the end of the Bible, or Ragnarök?'

'You mean Revelation? The end of times?'

'Yes. And there's a group that is reviving old spiritual practices. Like sun-worship. They're calling it a rebirthing for the planet.'

'People are looking for answers, huh?'

Terry nods.

Only one person notices us, a child in the rear passenger seat of a car packed with camping gear, who turns to stare. When I wave, she grins, and I can't help smiling back.

'Clear this side,' Terry says.

I wait for a gap between a refrigerated double-decker and a tourist bus to put my foot to the floor. The ATV's tyres grip on the bitumen and we gather speed as we cross. The drop between the highway and the gravel road on the other side is enough to launch us into the air. Terry grips the roll bar with both hands, knuckles white. The seats are already hard after the hours on the road, and the landing jars us to the bone, knocking all the air from our lungs. It shocks us into laughter, once we have established that nothing is broken and the ATV is still functional.

The forest closes around us. We're into the Pilliga.

AMATEUR TWILIGHT

The Pilliga

Gamilaraay Country

24:15:00

I FOLLOW ONE OF the old bird routes. The signposts used to lead twitchers and tourists through a series of backroads, giving them the best chance of seeing the two hundred and thirty species of birds that once inhabited the Pilliga Forest: red capped robins, glossy black cockatoos, brown tree creepers, dozens of honeyeaters. Dad said he and his little brother ticked off nearly two hundred during a weekend camping trip when he first got his licence. They drove up from Sydney especially. Most of those birds are on a different list now, crossed off for good.

Dark trunks flash by, a mix of ironbarks, white and black cypress undersown with wattles, still in fluffy yellow flower. Red dust billows out behind us, filling the open cab, working its way into every crevice. Terry is hunched up in the passenger seat, his fleece pulled up over his face.

'Try the goggles,' I say, pointing at the glovebox. 'Protect your eyes.'

He adjusts the strap and slips them over his head, kicking the glovebox closed with his boot.

'Better?'

He nods, leaning forward like my copilot in one of those war planes in old movies. In different circumstances, it would be comical. There would be pleasure, too, in showing someone my world. The red dust is Pilliga sandstone, ground down. That sandstone is the foundation for everything that happened. The vast layers of sediment laid down during the Jurassic, sand compressed and cemented into rock. Only to be shattered by the volcanic eruptions that threw up the Warrumbungle and Nandewar ranges. Now the sandstone is thinning, washed by water and torn by tools and tyres.

'Where were you born?' I say.

'Perth,' he says.

'What was that like?' In my mind, cities are all skyscrapers, shopping malls and bright artificial light, places without night.

'A mix of new and really old buildings. Lots of water. A park, with rows of tall trees and brown grass. Wide roads.' He shrugs. 'That was all from the window. I didn't leave our apartment until I was five.'

'Inside that whole time?'

'Yes.'

I shake my head. Just being in a classroom for forty minutes did my head in.

'A prisoner in your own life,' I say.

'I wasn't a prisoner. I was sick.'

'It's just a metaphor.'

Terry turns. 'What do you mean?'

'When you compare one thing with another to kind of make a point. Or express a bigger idea. It's not literal.'

'Okay,' Terry says.

It used to drive Hild and me nuts that the younger kids at school didn't understand us. They were almost illiterate in nature, which you couldn't blame them for, but it was more than that. Language itself was changing.

Something large moves in my peripheral view.

I throw my arm out in front of Terry. 'Emu!'

A father escorting two precious young, like stripy chooks on long legs. His head bobs forward as he runs, so strange and ungainly. For a moment we're travelling side by side, and then he leads his family away, down a side trail.

Both corners of Terry's mouth turn up. 'I didn't believe they were real,' he says.

Too soon, trees give way to dirty scars and a brown haze. We're into the gasfields, a sea of shiny pipelines and well heads, murky grey pools. Jets of flame roar high in the air, uncapped. The stink of it sticks in my throat and stings my eyes.

High fences and bright company signs can't hide the abandoned farmhouses and bare paddocks. Hectare after hectare of tree skeletons, stumps, and dried-up dams.

Dianella said there were families who could light the water coming out of their taps, farmers who could set fire to their creeks. She was away for ten days, recording their stories and photographing the evidence. When she got home, she barely spoke. Her skin broke out in a rash and a strange stomach upset saw her drop from lean to skinny over the next month. Dad made lasagne, and Stella dropped around fresh fruit and apple-and-cinnamon muffins, trying to bring her back to strength.

A flash of red, a fox slipping into a collapsed corrugated iron shed, is the only living thing. Token forest remnants are torched black, not even a blade of grass regrowing. Terry's goggled head moves back and forth, taking it all in, but there is no comment or reaction. Out here, he's stronger than I am, not knowing how it was before.

Everyone has their tipping point. The thing that pushes them over a threshold from which they can never return.

Dad had lived in Canberra before, when he was finishing his PhD. There was still a residence out at Mount Stromlo then, two great telescopes and the best astronomical library in the southern hemisphere. His team helped automate the first fully robotic telescope, which could message them updates, like a person.

The last message the telescope sent was just ahead of the Canberra fires, saying that the temperature was off the charts.

Dad described that fire as fluid, roaring and crackling out of the pine forest and breaking over the mountain like a wave. He was first on site. Whatever was left of the talking telescope was in the rubble, entombed beneath its charred steel dome. He said that although he'd never been in a battle, warzone was what came to mind.

The walls of the library were still smoking. He went inside, though he knew he shouldn't, to see if anything could be salvaged. Initially, the pages of all the books appeared intact, like some sort of miracle. But when he reached for one, a gust of wind blew through, and all the books turned to ash, right in front of him.

When he finally came home, his clothes, his hair, his face, were ghost-white. Dianella said that something in him changed that day, as if his own molecular structure was altered by the fierceness of that fire, and their powerlessness against it.

Before Black Summer or Black Spring, before we lived in the park, they thought it was going to happen all over again. The Wambelong megafire came charging up the escarpment towards the observatory, the sky roiling with smoke. Planes dropped water from the air. The staff who stayed to fight could see the flames closing in on the main telescope. It was only luck that the rusty old water tower, which no one had even thought to check for years, actually worked. And they were able to hold the fire back until the wind changed. The telescopes were safe.

But some of the outbuildings, including the original head astronomer's residence, were destroyed. In the pictures it looks like a bomb had been dropped. The fire raged on, for forty-one days, right through the park, taking all but the deepest gullies and highest corners.

It doesn't seem right that grand telescopes, trained on stars and planets millions of lightyears away, should be so vulnerable to forces on Earth – gods having to watch their feet when they walk. But like the old digital cameras, telescopes are based on mirrors. Maybe those who look closely at the origin of stars, into the past, are not in the best position to see the future.

If stars are questions, the answers tell us about ourselves.

23:03:00

I TAKE THE NEXT turnoff, tracking north. The ATV slides across the loose gravel and judders over deep corrugations. The sun is dropping, and the fuel gauge, too. The ATV is so much slower than a road vehicle – and less efficient. The battery doesn't seem to be charging properly. At the rate we're moving, it will be nearly dark by the time we get into camp.

I pull over next to a straggling stand of cypress pines. Once the dust settles, I leap out without opening the door. The fuel drums are heavy and covered in red dust. I open the tank and carefully unscrew the lid of a drum. It's a struggle to hold it on an angle long enough to empty the fuel, trying not to let in any dirt. I prop my leg on the sidestep and prop the drum on my leg to pour the diesel. A little drips onto my hand and down my wrist. I find a rag in the door pocket to wipe it off, but the smell remains.

Terry makes a tentative path behind a thin line of half-dead callitris. I head in the other direction, stepping over a single hyacinth orchid amid a tangle of weeds at the road's edge. A copse of tiny wattles has self-seeded, the start of some sort of recovery.

We can't be far from Dandry Gorge. If I could camp anywhere, it would be in the shelter of that sandstone valley. Turquoise parrots, yellow robins and black cockatoos hang on near the sandy creek beds, where water still runs deep underneath; you just have to dig. Cycads, those living fossils, among black cypress and bloodwoods, even rusty figs in the wettest places. The ridgelines have a view all around, so you can see what's coming. Or that's how I remember it. It's a place I dream about; somewhere that could be home.

Down on the flat, I can't see much further than the road stretching away ahead of us and behind us. And the grey gasfields either side.

I stretch my shoulders and quads while Terry washes his hands, swatting at flies and fidgeting with his clothes. I'm tired and empty but too nervy to be hungry. And I don't want to eat in this place.

'Okay to keep going?' I say. 'It should only be another hour or so.'

'Yes,' Terry says.

We climb back into the ATV for the last leg of a long day on the road. The ATV turns over, coughs, and stalls.

'What's wrong with it?' Terry says.

'The fuel, maybe.' I try the ignition again. And again, it turns over, coughs, and does not start. *Great.*

We could probably have just made it to the tower with what was in the tank, which would have been a lot better than being stuck here. I could have completed the second of my pointless tasks, at least. I try one more time.

'Please,' I say.

The engine coughs and backfires, blows black smoke, and this time it starts.

Terry lets out an exaggerated sigh of relief and slides his goggles back on. I hold out my hand for a high five. He hesitates, and then touches my palm. His fingers are soft and pink.

I start easy in the loose sand and slalom my way back onto the road. Only once I slot into the tracks of a vehicle that has gone before us can I push the accelerator flat to the floor. We're a cloud of engine noise and red dust moving towards the Forest Tower.

It was months after Dad died before I saw the photographs Dianella took from that rooftop in Parkes. I kept checking the family file, but she hadn't uploaded them. I guess it didn't feel so much like a family anymore.

Eventually I went looking for myself. I had memorised her laptop password, initially to forge emails to the deputy principal explaining my absences when Hild and I needed to bust out or I was spending the day with Uncle Nate. She hadn't changed it. While she was in yet another meeting with Blair and Des, I logged in to access her files.

The Parkes pictures, as they were labelled, were not of the sky at all, but avenues of streetlights and warehouses, trucks and trains, eerie middle-of-the-night spaces. She'd been out roaming, like a cat. As far as Murriyang, the old radio telescope in the paddocks on the edge of town: 'The Dish' as it was affectionately known, a symbol of Australia's contribution to the *Apollo 11* mission. Why was our astronomy always in service of America?

Dianella's images of the hospital were a sick green. She had highlighted the very window, in a wall of windows, where I had been sitting with Dad, with the lights of the town around it eerie and strange, as if on some distant planet.

Dianella *never* featured in her own photos. Occasionally she had put me in a shot, for scale, or when lacking an interesting foreground. But the final picture was a single timer shot of her sitting by the metal ladder on the edge of the rooftop garden, a dead potted palm beside her, framed by white LED light. If I hadn't just seen her walk out the door, I would have taken it for a suicide note.

The image of Dianella sitting there alone, broke something in me. I sat in front of her screen, sobbing. And I had no choice but to try to forgive my mother for not being there all those nights, while I watched the starlight fade from my father.

My parents' world was large, a cosmos. I grew up orbiting them, and the three of us made a high-functioning team. But as the Dark Skies dimmed, my parents' powers dwindled.

The Thinning

As they were less, we were less. And once Dad was sick, we were less still.

With him gone, nothing fits back together in the same way. My mother and I are stuck, orbiting each other like binary stars, a dark nebula of loss, devoted to the project of survival.

21:17:00

THE STEEL LEGS OF the Forest Tower glint in late sun. It replaced the old tower, which, in turn, had replaced a wooden structure lost in bushfires when it was all state forest. The new tower was built with tourists in mind: wide steps with safety railings, leading up to a broad viewing platform. It's only a hundred metres up, on top of the rocky outcrop above the campground, but the land being so flat all around affords the view I remember.

We putter past the row of sites tucked into the trees. When I was a kid, there were only ever a few other campers. But a day out from the eclipse, the sites are all occupied by off-road vans and four-wheel drives towing camper-trailers. Some are brand-new, high-end, probably on their maiden voyage. Others are more makeshift, homemade ute conversions, all welded steel plates and compartments. The survivalist model, as Dad called them.

We're late into camp; everyone is already sitting around their fires. Couples preparing meals watch us pass by. One has a toddler. There are no other children. Terry leaves his goggles on until we reach the last spot in the row, farthest from the tower, which is empty. It isn't as private as I'd like, visible from the neighbouring site. We're also the only ones in a tent, which feels like a very thin membrane.

Terry unloads while I set up. The ATV's coiled shock absorbers and underbelly are thick with red Pilliga dust.

The previous campsite inhabitant has left a gift: a pile of split, kiln-dried ironbark and a handful of callitris kindling. I gather a clutch of leaves and a crumpled brown paper bag from the edge of the clearing. Terry watches me strike a match and the flames take hold. Breathing in the fragrant oils feels like home.

My ears are ringing from the engine, and my skin itchy with red dust. I'd kill for a hot shower, but a quick wash will have to do.

I hand Terry the water bottles. 'Fill those at the tank near the toilets? There's a track along there through the trees.'

'Okay.'

Our neighbours watch him go. I lift my chin in greeting. 'Hey.'

'Evening,' the woman says. But she does not smile.

There is no service in camp. That much hasn't changed. But there will be from up on the tower. I walk out to the edge of our clearing. The sun is setting but there is no one up top.

When Terry returns, water spilt over the front of his shirt, our neighbours again watch his progress.

I place larger pieces of wood on the fire, allowing plenty of airflow. Soon it's roaring, really putting out some heat, which we're going to need. I fill the billy with water and set it over the first coals. Once it has boiled, I use a little of the water and one of the tiny washers my mother knitted to wash my face, neck and hands. Terry is squirming, scratching at his skin, brushing off his clothes. I hand him the other washer, which I would normally use for dishes, and my cleanser.

'You should wash your face,' I say. 'All that dust.'

'I feel like it is inside my ears.'

'It probably is.'

I moisturise my face and hands and offer him the little jar. His expressions as he tries to rub it in are comical. Something about the position of his eyebrows and everything being such a struggle.

I empty the dehydrated goat tagine into the cooker and cover it with water.

'Let's go up the tower for sunset while this soaks,' I say.

'Okay.'

I get the feeling it's more that he doesn't want to be left alone in camp, but he won't be sorry. We put on our fleeces and beanies and follow the narrow track past the other campers to the cluster of covered tables, barbecues and toilets around a large clearing. The red soil almost glows in the late light. I take the track winding around to the tower and Terry follows.

'Another cave?' He peers into the dark of the opening.

'The Salt Caves,' I say. 'It used to be deeper, with stalactites and everything. Gamilaraay used it as a shelter. And animals came to lick the salt.'

'Lick it?'

'For the minerals.'

He leans inside and, for a moment, I think he's going to taste the cave wall for himself. Instead, he clicks his fingers, turning his head one way, and then the other. A breeze caresses my cheek and then is gone.

'Can we go inside?' he says.

'We don't want to miss the sunset,' I say. And the cave has always unnerved me. It's like photography; the shadows contain all the noise.

'It leads somewhere.'

'What do you mean?'

'There's an opening at the back.'

'Huh,' I say.

We start the climb, the wind whispering around our ears. The steps are just metal grating, allowing a view to the ground, if you look. Terry is looking. And now he's freezing up.

'Focus on your hands, not your feet,' I say.

The sun is sinking fast. I don't want to miss it, but I'm scared of what we'll see, too. Of erasing the story that I've built myself around. My thighs are burning by the time we reach the top. The last of the sun is side-lighting the forest and tinting the underside of the clouds pink.

I've prepared myself, but it's still a gut punch: the extent of the gas fires, the spread of the open-cut mines, like a pox or plague, great holes surrounded by vast stretches of dirt scraped bare. What was neverending forest is now a tiny island, all its edges visible. But what is left is still wild, still beautiful. Dark trunks in red sand, deep rooted. And the greatwater, far below, still breathing in and out, with the forest.

Tonight, the Dark Emu will still fly overhead; the galactic core still holds the universe together.

When I look back, towards the Warrumbungles, I feel the gravitational pull of home, but my centre is all stretched out of shape. Terry clings to the handrail like his life depends on it, making his way around to stand beside me.

'That's where we were,' I say, pointing to the silhouette of the Warrumbungles. I spin around. 'And that's where we're going.' The Nandewar Range awaits, as enigmatic as ever, in the opposite direction.

I hand him the binoculars. 'Have a look.'

'We'll be there tomorrow morning?' he says.

'We'd better be,' I say.

While Terry's eyes are behind three layers of lenses, I check the roof. There are more antennae than I remember. The tower is just one in a series of towers, monitoring weather and fire conditions. The steel compartment is still up there, high enough that I can't see into it from the floor of the viewing platform.

'I think I can see the big telescope,' Terry says.

'Anything else?'

'The heli is in the air.'

Images come in a rush: Jade and Pete sprinting uphill in the gloom, Pete just in front. And my mother, stumbling, her hands empty. Why doesn't she have her camera? And why aren't I there with them, instead of here, looking back from a distance?

Even in Dianella's childhood photos she was holding a camera. Vernon gave her the first, an old Leicaflex, when she was eight. She was hooked from the start, documenting family ski trips and snowshoe expeditions at home as well as in Norway, Finland and Japan. I can imagine Vernon having to wrestle the camera from her, even then, to include her in the frame. In those images, her face is carefree. She says there were years, maybe her whole childhood, when she was oblivious to change, like the ice retreating beneath their skis.

Those family photos, despite all the hand-knitted woollen jumpers, don't look warm. Her parents are never holding her, or each other. And I can't help feeling that their smiles would have faded as soon as the photo was taken.

The camera has always been Dianella's way of charting her course, making her own life, making a difference. I can't imagine her without it.

20:07:00

IT'S DARK WHEN WE get back to camp. Terry helps me drag a log closer to the fire and we sit down to warm our hands. I use a stick to level the coals and place two new pieces of wood at the edges, fill the billy and set it on the logs to boil. As soon as the water is bubbling, I pull it off the heat and pour enough over the couscous to cover it.

'Right,' I say. 'Let's heat up this goat.'

'Goat!'

'You ate some already. That curry back at camp.'

'Well, I'm so hungry I *could* eat a goat,' he says.

'Wait. Was that meant to be a joke?'

Terry smiles, and for a moment he's just a kid by a campfire. I light the cooker, add hot water and stir the tagine as it heats through. I keep adding water, a little at a time, and stirring until the meat chunks are soft, the vegetables plump.

I spoon couscous into two bowls, then the steaming tagine on top. My mouth is already watering. I hand Terry the larger bowl and a fork, and we shovel food into our mouths.

'How old are you?' I say.

'Fourteen.'

'So you're second-gen?'

'Yes. Number twelve hundred and thirty-nine,' he says. 'But the first with other abilities. On the record, anyway. I'm known as E1.'

'What do you mean by on the record?'

'More of us have been born than are registered.'

'Homebirths or they hide the baby?'

'Or got rid of it.'

'That's messed up.'

Terry nods.

The tagine is so rich and spicy, I'm eating too fast again. I put my fork down and push a piece of wood into the centre of the fire with my boot.

'So, let me get this straight. Your parents were planning to take off before these NASA people actually arrived?'

'The rest of the team was staying for the handover. No one could have known we were leaving.'

'Except that one friend, who owns the house on the island. And whoever was driving the vehicle at the checkpoints.'

'You think one of them betrayed us?'

'Maybe. How did your parents communicate with them?'

'Encrypted app,' he says. 'What do you think has happened to them?'

I scrape up my last mouthfuls and chew slowly. 'Don't take this the wrong way, but I think they'll want them alive. To get to you. And it sounds like they have expertise that's in high demand right now.'

Terry stares into the flames. 'What are your mother and the others going to do?'

I take his empty bowl and stack it on top of mine. 'I'm not sure. Take control of the observatory, she said.'

'With eight people?'

'I know. There must be more to it,' I say. 'I kind of thought our tasks were pointless –'

'To get rid of me.'

I nod. 'But what if they do need us? For their plan to work.'

'I don't think your mother would ask you to do anything for no reason.'

I can't help laughing. 'You don't know her like I do.'

Terry watches me put more wood on the fire and boil water for tea and washing up.

'You camped here with your parents?'

'A long time ago.'

We turn at the scuffling of an animal in the undergrowth behind us.

'Have you heard about Rambo, the fox who lived here, in the Pilliga scrub?'

Terry looks up, firelight reflecting on his glasses. 'No.'

'He was on Australia's Most Wanted list for years.'

'Is he a really a fox? Or is this a metaphor?'

I smile. 'He really was a fox. The most elusive fox in the

world, outsmarting rangers, hunters, trackers and scientists for years,' I say. 'Rambo's mother was killed in a trap when he was just a kit. And his brother picked up a bait – poison they put out for feral animals. Rambo survived somehow, on his own. He was wary of people and he was smart. He didn't stick to the cycles of the moon like other foxes. He didn't fall for baits or snares or traps. He never used the same path twice.

'National Parks and the Nature Conservancy had set up a sanctuary, a fenced area where they were going to reintroduce bilbies, bettongs, bandicoots, wallabies and western quolls. They weren't extinct then, just regionally extinct. But the whole program was on hold because of Rambo. He was inside the fence.

'A bloke called Sparrow, as tall as a tree, was in charge of catching Rambo.'

'Sparrow is a man? Chasing Rambo, who is a real fox.'

'Yes,' I say. 'An actual man. He set up hidden infrared cameras, traps and lure boxes, and sat up all night himself with a thermal rifle. They'd catch Rambo on film, staring right into the camera, as if he knew it was there. Sparrow brought in Indigenous trackers, ex-military assassins, soft-jaw-trap specialists, and hunters with specially-bred tracker dogs. Rambo evaded them all.'

Terry leans forwards, elbows on knees. 'How?'

'Foxes can see six times better than humans. Their sense of smell is ten thousand times better than ours. Not to mention hearing. And they can sense electromagnetic fields – who knows what else. So probably the cameras, all that metal and plastic, the lithium batteries, gave it away. Sparrow would shower, use no products at all, wash his clothes in unscented detergent, and still Rambo smelt him a mile off. Sparrow started dreaming about that fox, every night, and could sense when he was near.'

'Rambo sensed him, too.'

'Exactly,' I say. 'They had a connection. Everything Sparrow tried, Rambo just knew, and changed his habits again.'

'What happened?'

'Well, after five years on the run, evading thousands of traps and baits, hundreds of stakeouts, fifty days of scent-tracking dogs hot on his trail and a hundred cameras filming for forty hours a week, it was water that got him. After the floods out here, Rambo disappeared. Three months went by without a single sighting. And Sparrow stopped dreaming about Rambo.

'Parks introduced the greater bilbies to the enclosure. No fox. The bilbies thrived and were released into the forest. For the first time in a century, they lived wild in the Pilliga. Then Parks went through the same process for the bridled nail-tail wallabies and brush-tailed bettong, and then the vulnerable plains mouse and western barred bandicoot. For a time, they all lived here again.'

'Are they still here?' Terry's voice is small and quiet, like one of those marsupials.

Tears have come up from nowhere, the way they do sometimes. I blink them away and swallow. 'Bilbies have lived here for fifteen million years, so I'm hoping some have hung on.'

'But foxes have adapted better,' Terry says.

18:07:00

I WRIGGLE AROUND ON my thermarest, trying to get comfortable. Terry is already asleep, releasing little puffs of air as his chest goes up and down in the sleeping bag.

I love sleeping outside but sometimes I do miss my bed, my room, and all the things in it: my books and maps, my watercolour pencils, my headphones, my feather collection. Having an actual house with doors that close and rooms that you cannot see unless you walk into them, a bathroom. Still feeling Dad's presence: his bird books, telescopes, star charts and detective novels. 'Brain the size of a galaxy, and he reads that crap,' my mother would say.

I miss Dianella's photographs on the walls, even after seeing them a million times. And walking into her studio while she was working, when she used to smile and show me what the camera had captured, rather than shutting her laptop and sending me away.

There was a stage when I took photographs, too, with one of Dianella's old cameras. The files will be among hers somewhere. I experimented with macro shots and wide-angle landscapes – all in daylight. But eventually I returned to the dark, messing around with star trails. They took longer to get right, experimenting with ISO and exposure times up to an hour, and having to make sure the camera was pointing true north. But the swirl of stars and colour showing Earth's rotation was mesmerising. I only had one image printed and framed, at Dianella's request. I found her in my room looking at it once. She put her hand on my shoulder but said nothing.

I planned it months out. A clear night when all the telescopes would be in use on a new moon. It took forever to get the tripod steady and frame the shot, perched there on the slope, out in front of the telescopes, looking back at them. A hundred images at thirty seconds each, which I stacked and processed myself. The telescopes' hatches are wide open, pointed upwards, their great square mouths gulping down the stars and their trails. Like we gulped them down. The same way we gulp everything down.

My passion for photographing the night sky died with Dianella's – with Dad, maybe. But I am proud of that photo. The transformation that I captured and the transformation of capturing it.

Still, there is a freedom in travelling light, without all the possessions and habits that tie us down. It's safer, too, carrying everything you need on your own back, being able to move on in a moment.

The day Dianella and I left the residence, deciding what to take was so overwhelming that I took almost nothing. Not one book and not even the bracelet Hild bought me for my sixteenth.

When I last looked, the residence was as we left it, the windows dusty and cornered with webs. I still carry a key on the chain around my neck, but never risked going in.

Maybe one of those soldiers, or whoever they are, the heli pilot maybe, is sleeping in my bed right now, using my desk to read their messages and scan reports. Cooking with our pots and pans, reading our books, and looking at the things on our walls. Or not looking, I guess. Not caring.

Anger rises in me, hot and red. Why should they be occupying our home, the observatory, the telescopes? They probably don't even know whose Country it is.

I wasn't listening properly when Uncle Nate said goodbye. There was anger in him when he said they were going to 'put an end to all this'. What would that even mean? I can't go there, in my mind. It's too much.

And I need sleep, not more questions. I picture the spring, my rockpool, the moment of immersing my body in cold water, the number of white spots on the black flanks of an adult diamond firetail, like stars in a dark sky, and try to breathe my way back to calm.

16:50:00

THE TOWER WAKES ME. The wind singing in the scaffolding, the metal contracting in the cold, and the hum of radio instruments reminds me of the telescopes creaking and turning at home.

I sit up in my sleeping bag and reach into my pack for Dianella's black box. I hold it to my chest, listening for Terry's deep breathing before I wriggle free, unzip the tent and step outside. It's cold and quiet. I'm turning into my mother, sneaking around in the middle of the night, trusting no one.

I pad along the sand, waiting for my eyes to adjust. People think of darkness as an absence of light but it's the other way around. Light is only darkness diluted. Even true night, total darkness, has nuances once your eye adjusts. Once you train yourself to see.

Still, walking at night was easier in starlight. And the stars' position and movement were a guide. Not just for us. Turtles, bats, migratory birds, whales and insects all used them to navigate. Like the bogong moths, on their great migration back to the high country. Without their skymap, they were lost.

They turned up in the park one year, at dusk. Ilse drove around, asking all the caravaners to turn off their lights. But the moths flew into our lamps and candles, getting stuck in the wax. Their fat content was so high, they burned hot and bright.

I gaze up at the tower, the Dark Emu faint, but climbing behind it. Even without Dianella, I'm still framing the shot: the azimuthal of the galactic core, composition, visibility, exposure. It's a process embedded at a cellular level.

Alpha and Beta Centauri are a little lower than last night. The stars move through the night but also shift one degree every day, like a great clock. A clock that is counting down.

I can't really look at Beta without thinking of my family. The three-star system we used to be, and the two-star arrangement we're in now. Dad said once that there are rogue planets and stars, not in our solar system, but beyond, who can break free, or are flung out of, the gravitational pull of their binary systems.

Betel blinks or shivers. Something passes between us.

'Hey, Betel. Coming your way.'

The railing is too cold to touch, the whole tower shaking in the wind. The hundred metres seems much higher now. I pull my neck warmer up over my mouth and nose and keep going, one step at a time. Since we left the park, I've been trying to see inside Dianella's black box, to guess what images she chose to preserve. The ones she thought were her best? Like the full extent of the Milky Way arched over the red lunettes of Lake Mungo.

Or the most significant events? Like all the explosive colours of each stage of Betel turning supernova, changing our night skies forever. Or the ones that document the fifty thousand objects launched into space since I was born? There is a weight to them, that's for sure.

When I reach the top, I set the box down on the platform. The other puzzle is the combination. Who else has it? Is there a clue on the box itself, some number sequence I'm meant to know or guess? If it was another of Dianella's problems to solve, I've failed. I attach the recordings I've made so far to the top of the box with duct tape, my hands clumsy.

The metal cavity is high in the apex of the roof, well out of sight and reach, which is a good thing. But how do I get the box up there? It's getting heavier by the minute.

I hold it by the handle and use my other hand to pull myself up and stand on the railing. I edge along, gripping the strut above. Between the tower shifting in the wind, and the numbness in my hands, it's precarious. But I get myself into position, in front of the cavity. If I lean out, and could hold the box horizontal in front of me, I could throw it in. But it's too heavy, and too far.

There's a sound far below. I freeze, gripping cold metal. Someone is on the tower, their uneven steps coming up the stairs. I'm shivering, my body heat draining away, and my strength with it. There is no way to avoid being seen and I can't think of a plausible story to explain myself. I tense my body, ready to kick or to use the box as a weapon.

When I risk peeking down, it's Terry's pale moon face looking up.

I empty my lungs of breath before whispering. 'What are you doing?'

He holds up a rope. 'I remembered this, under my seat.'

I smile, though my skin is so tight in the cold dry air, it hurts my face. 'Perfect,' I say.

Terry holds the box, resting its weight on the railing, while I throw the rope over the centre strut. I tie one end to the handle of the box and raise it until it's level with the shelf.

I hand Terry the rope. 'Okay. Hold this tight. Just keep the tension on it.'

With Terry taking the weight, I can lean right out and push the box into the slot and release the rope. It takes three attempts, but we do it. My arms are shaking when I climb down from the rail, and I'm grateful for Terry's shoulder to steady me.

We descend in silence. At the bottom, Terry gazes up at the stars, their light reflected in his eyes. We fox-walk past the campsites, teeth chattering, tensing for someone to have woken, but there is no sound or movement.

It's only when we're back in the tent, zipped into our sleeping bags, beginning to thaw, that I can speak.

'How did you know?'

Terry shifts his legs. 'Well, I heard what your mother said to you. And I ... kind of felt you planning, when we were up there. Where to put the box.'

'What, you can read minds?'

'It's a process of logic,' he says. 'But I get a sense sometimes, a picture.'

I let out a low whistle. 'This is why they really want you.'

'I think so.' There is sadness in his voice.

11:12:00

I'M UP AND OUT of the tent before the sun. She's still resting, ahead of her big day. I rekindle the fire and spark up the cooker. I need hot tea to warm my hands – and fast. There is a light frost on the ATV and the fly of the tent.

A magpie lands in a branch above to inspect my work. His claws are enormous. Maybe it's a Pilliga thing, to deal with bigger prey.

Our neighbour is up, too, in matching aqua gloves and beanie, tufts of grey hair sticking out at angles. He's trying to catch my eye as hard as I'm trying to avoid his.

The magpie throws back his head and chortles a tune, the local variation on morning song.

'Hey, Maggie,' I say. 'Do you know there's going to be a total eclipse today?'

Mr Nosy looks over, hoping I'm talking to him. Thankfully, another camper chooses that moment to step through the screen of trees.

'Heading up for the eclipse?' the man says.

'We booked our spot at base camp three years ago,' Mr Nosy says. 'This is our thirteenth eclipse.'

I drop the lid of the cooker. Of course. The whole thing will be ticketed and policed. Maggie swoops down and settles on the log next to me. He is a male, as I thought, his white feathers extending further down his back. Maggie looks into my eyes and tilts his head. My blood rushes, my skin tingles. There is something about an animal looking back at us, the same way we look at them.

Mr Nosy shifts his weight and scans our campsite, muttering something under his breath. The other man's reply is too quiet to hear. Maggie flies across the clearing, and swoops. Mr Nosy take a step back, waves his arms above head and disappears back inside the caravan.

The campground has a weird energy, but I can't quite put my finger on what it is.

Terry emerges from the tent. His face is blank and sleepy until he slips on his glasses.

'Morning,' I say.

'Morning, Fin.'

'You heard?'

Terry nods. 'There are going to be a lot of people.'

'I don't think we'll be able to drive up the mountain,' I say. 'I wish I'd thought of that yesterday. We'd better get moving.'

I detach the fly from the tent and throw it over the ATV to dry while we finish packing. The sun is up and I'm relishing its warmth on my face. People are still having their breakfast when I walk back to the picnic area to wash our dishes and refill the water bottles. Maggie follows me, shifting from tree to tree. I've offered him a strip of jerky, which he pecked at. But he's fussing around, as if to hurry me. Like the instrument on my wrist isn't already keeping time.

Our neighbours are climbing the tower. To check in with family, probably, but I watch until they reach the top. They're taking pictures of the view, not looking up at the black box. If Mr Nosy doesn't spot it, no one will. Unless they know where to look. Mrs Nosy peers down at us, then lifts her device to her ear. My breakfast threatens to come back up. It could be nothing, but that's not the feeling.

It's only since leaving the park that I've had to think about how I'm perceived. What the narrative is around people like me. Illegals and Absconders, as the government calls us. And especially people like Terry. We are *other*, outsiders.

Maggie sounds the alarm. It's too cold for a snake or goanna. I scan for a fox or dingo. There is nothing, but I shift up a gear, scrunching my sleeping bag back in its bag, deflating and rolling the thermarest, packing it into its little case. Terry watches my technique and packs up his side of the tent. Quicker and neater than yesterday morning in the park. Was that really only yesterday?

I shove things in bags and shove the bags in the ATV, then jog back to the picnic area to fill my water bottle. I've been trying not to look at the bright watch face but I can feel the seconds ticking by.

A face appears at the window of one of the caravans and then disappears. A woman my age. I stop. That's what's missing: girls and young women. Maggie is flapping his wings and calling.

'What is it?' I say. 'What do you want me to do?'

I'm screwing on the lid of the bottle when I hear the vehicle. I walk back to the trailhead, trying to look casual, and glance over my shoulder. It's a white four-wheel drive, covered in red dust, with the National Parks' insignia. Three uniforms inside. They could be here to clean the toilets, do some maintenance, any number of mundane things that have nothing to do with us or Mrs Nosy. With the eclipse so close, perhaps they're checking bookings. Campers always have been keen to save a few dollars. And with Illegals unable to book and pay online, there is a new edge to their policing.

My heart is thumping as I stride back to our site. I've never quite mastered the art of appearing relaxed but holding your body coiled, ready to act.

'Time to go,' I say, in a cheery voice.

Maggie is there ahead of me, perched on the roll bar of the ATV. And Terry, bless him, reads the situation. He throws the last of our gear in the back while I fold the fly and lifts himself into the passenger seat.

The ATV starts first try but I wince at the noise. In an electric vehicle, we could have crept away. We could go right past the rangers, and head straight out to the highway. Instead, I pootle down the road in the opposite direction, towards the dam, as if we have all the time in the world. I can only hope they don't come after us, and that by the time they work their way along each of the sites and reach our nosy neighbours for a chat, we'll be long gone.

The dam used to be one of Dad's favourite birdwatching sites. The water level is low, not a single bird in sight. But for a moment I think I see Dad lying on the bank, binoculars to his eyes, watching grebes bicker. And maybe he is with us somehow, because my body is still doing things even though I'm scared.

Terry puts on his goggles as we pick up speed. He turns to look behind us.

'Anything?'

'A ranger is standing on the road, near where we were camped,' Terry says. 'She's looking this way.'

'Shit.'

'Oh, no,' Terry says.

'What?'

'She's getting in the vehicle. They're coming after us.'

'Fuck.'

The road peters out ahead of us, and a tree has fallen or been placed across it. I was sure there used to be a connection through to the route north. There is still a bit of a goat track, enough for us to continue, and hope that the Parks troopy can't or won't follow. And the downed tree is only a young cypress pine. I accelerate. Terry grips the roll bar as we lurch up, over and down the other side. I dodge rocks and fallen timber, branches thwack against the side of the vehicle and scratch my arm. A lone male grey kangaroo hops away, into the trees. I catch a glimpse of colour, a scattering of wildflowers worthy of my full attention, but they're just a blur.

Terry looks back. 'They've stopped at the log,' he says. 'They're arguing. And the bird is there.'

'The magpie?'

'Black and white bird, from camp. He's swooping them.'

'Huh,' I say. 'Hang on.' I put my foot to the floor, to put as much distance as possible between us and them. To make following us and risking damage to a government vehicle seem futile and undesirable. We lurch around a bend, to clearer ground, the old road visible again ahead of us. We've reached the edge of the national park, heading back into what used to be state forest.

'I can't see them anymore,' Terry says.

'Yeah!' I hold up my hand for a high five, and this time Terry smacks my palm. I take three deep breaths and relax my shoulders. That magpie – so weird. But *thank you*.

It was Dad's presence I felt, but it's my mother I'm thinking of. All those pointless tasks that I resented so much. They were to teach me to act, to take calculated risks in a moment just like this, when neither of them would be around.

NAUTICAL TWILIGHT

Narrabri

Gamilaraay Country

09:02:00

I TAKE THE TURN off onto Pilliga Forest Way. Whenever I accelerate, we slip-slide all over the road in loose sand, so it has to be slow and steady, trying to ignore the time ticking by. A dark object appears on the road ahead, too low to be a kangaroo or wallaby, and it doesn't run away as we approach. We're almost upon it before I recognise the dirty black of a feral pig. It skulks off, into the scrub. Terry stares after it. It doesn't behave like pigs should behave. Shooters used to release piglets into the parks on purpose and now they have the run of the place.

Too soon, the forest peters out into logged coupes. A few saplings persist among strewn timber and blackened ground. Dust billows off a string of abandoned strip mines. Then we're back into another expanse of gasfields, belching and flaming. Fracking is like it sounds. Holes drilled down into the aquifers, toxic chemicals and explosives pumped in to shatter rock and release gas from deep underground. Eventually an error contaminated the Great Artesian Basin – the water supply for millions – accelerating a whole new wave of extinctions.

So much Country laid to waste is wearing on my senses. The only upside is that the roads are better, flattened by logging and mining trucks, and I can up the speed.

'How long?' Terry says.

I show him my watch without looking at it. At this rate it's a couple of hours to the base of the mountain. And then five hours to climb Kaputar and get into position. That's without factoring in hordes of people and dodging ticket checks. It's going to be tight.

The next turn takes us northeast again. At last it feels like we're heading towards our destination.

We pass the sign for the bore, another childhood camp spot, where we would watch birds morning and evening, and swim through the heat of the day. People used to travel from all over the country, all over the world, to bathe in the warm waters bubbling up from the Artesian Basin, which were thought to have healing properties. It did ease my knee injury from hockey, and warm water with extra buoyancy is always rejuvenating. For me it was more the ritual of immersing myself in waters from deep underground, from the Earth itself.

During those hours, my mother left her camera bag in the car. Splashing around in swimmers, there were no lenses, no tripods, no work to be done.

Dad jetted water at me through his closed fist. I tried to copy him, but my tiny burbles had no force.

'How do you do that?'

'You'll figure it out.'

I splashed him with both hands instead.

My mother dived down, did a headstand and walked forward, only her slender ankles and feet showing above the water. I threw myself towards her, to tickle her wrinkled toes.

She burst to the surface, giggling. 'Not fair.'

I swam away, stretching out into freestyle, pulling my hands hard through the water, back past my body, and kicking my legs in a steady four-beat, showing off the results of swim-training. When my hands touched the side, I stopped to look back. But my parents were entwined under water, smiling at each other.

'Can we go to the Pilliga Baths tomorrow?' I said.

My mother tipped her head. 'I was thinking Horton Falls.'

'Bit out of the way,' Dad said.

'I'll drive,' my mother said, holding her hands up, as if they were already at the wheel.

⸺

A quadbike tears out of a laneway in front of us, skids, and then roars up the road in a cloud of dust. Just a couple of guys pushing the limits. I didn't hear it coming over the noise of our own engine. I decelerate to let them pull away, hoping they're headed elsewhere. But the boy riding pillion turns around. And then they're doing a one-eighty, coming back.

I play it cool, nodding and raising two fingers from the steering wheel. But they've picked us as foreigners in their land. They ride straight at us, whooping and carrying on, swerving only at the last minute. I don't slow or brake or deviate from our path. The passenger, in a footy beanie, is filming the whole thing and who knows where that's going to end up.

They turn around and come after us again. My foot is flat to the floor but they run level with us, still filming. They cut in front, and I have to brake to avoid colliding with them, sending us into a sandbank. The ATV stalls. I restart and try to reverse out of the sand but the wheels are spinning.

The boys tear around and around, drowning us in dust. I get the ATV moving again but they are circling us in ever-smaller loop, cutting me off whenever I try to burst through, like a cattle dog. And they are animals, jeering and taunting. Terry's face is inscrutable but his knuckles are white on the dash. It's as if the boys sense that we cannot retaliate. We could disappear out here and no one would know. And no one would ever find us.

'Eat my dirt, cunts!' The driver is older, his head shaved. His grin makes my blood boil.

The ATV has more power; they have more manoeuvrability. But they are more vulnerable, too.

'Hang on,' I say.

Terry grips the roll bar with both hands. While they are behind us, I accelerate, angling hard across the road, so that they have to switch sides to come around again. Then I angle back the other way, accelerating out of the slide, hard-holding the juddering steering wheel. They come along side, just behind us and, this time, I continue to steer towards them, forcing them onto the edge of the road, where the dust is thick and deep, towards a clump of fallen timber. They have nowhere to go and drop back, swearing.

I keep my foot to the floor, leaving them to eat *our* dirt. The road is so straight that they remain in sight for a long time. Terry keeps checking over his shoulder, until at last we take a gentle bend and are free of them.

Terry sits back in his seat, shaking his head, as if he can't believe what just happened. And the further we drive, the less real it seems. Just a bad dream fading from memory. Or a warning, of what might be ahead.

08:09:02

I STICK TO THE backroads as long as I can, skirting the fenced edges of extraction sites and burnt-out forest. But to get to Kaputar, we have to do a stretch on the highway. Everything is too loud, too open, too fast. We swerve around a dead kangaroo on the verge, belly bloated, struck by a vehicle moving faster than ours. Terry puts his hands over his goggles.

A passing B-triple nearly blows us off the road. ATVs weren't meant for highways and the roads weren't built for trucks that big. For a moment, we're sucked into its slipstream, dragged closer and closer to its roaring wheels. I struggle for control, hair whipping around my face, gripping the steering wheel too tight. Terry braces. I can't think for the growl of rubber on bitumen, moving metal. Gravel spits up, spraying the little windscreen. I shut my eyes and lift my foot from the accelerator. We fall back, and then we're released.

We pass a highway patrol car, pulling over someone towing an overloaded trailer with no taillights. Another police vehicle flies past, heading in the opposite direction, lights flashing.

The paddocks either side of us are brown, the farmhouses run down and rambling.

'Do you even have a licence?' Terry says.

I shake my head. 'We're not in the system. Couldn't go for the test.' And although the ATV would have been registered once, I'm pretty sure it isn't now.

The fuel gauge is down to one-third. There is probably a way through the northeast corner of the Pilliga to the Kamilaroi Highway, where we need to get to, but I could waste a lot of time and fuel trying to find it, and then we might have to backtrack anyway. It would be so much quicker going through Narrabri. It's risky, but we're running out of time.

I lean towards Terry. 'It's only twenty ks to town,' I say. 'From there, we can skirt around, get to a backroad which takes us to the base of the mountain. Another hour, maybe. If we keep going cross-country, I'm just guessing.'

Terry looks at my watch and nods. 'There are risks on the backroads, too.'

A misshapen procession of vans, caravans, SUVs, utes and trailers laden with camping gear clog the slow lane. We're no longer the slowest, and far from the only strange sight. We pass a homemade caravan constructed from old packing crates, held together with wallpaper, staples and roof ties. For a time, we travel alongside a truck towing a glass tiny home with a family having a meal inside. Two older women on an antique motorbike with a sidecar roar past in retro helmets and goggles.

We pass a pair of cyclists on the verge, laden with heavy packs and panniers. They are the only people who wave. I'm wishing I could film the spectacle.

Like in the campsite, there are few girls and young women. There are dozens of the old pop-top electric campervans in retro colours that Hild and I dreamed of travelling around the country in. Mostly older couples or young men, but sometimes two women, and I catch myself envying not just their immaculate van fitouts, but their freedom. Most of all, I'm missing Hild – and regretting all the things I did not say.

Many of the vehicles are flying a long purple flag with what looks like a spiral helix symbol.

'Have you seen that before?' I say.

Terry shakes his head. He's counting down the kilometres out loud. We see only one more police car, behind us, lights flashing but no siren. I'm sure she's coming for us, and am already concocting my story, but she roars past in the outside lane. Terry and I glance at each other. It's as if we're invisible or some force is with us. So far, anyway.

We're not far from the Compact Array, the linked dishes working together to collect radio waves and turning them into images of objects in space. It was one of Dianella's aims to get a shot of all six telescopes beneath the Milky Way when it was horizontal in the sky. The night everything lined up, I couldn't go because we had a school excursion to the Brewarrina fish traps leaving early the next day.

It was the best excursion that year by far. I wished I'd taken a camera. The oldest human-built structures in the world, and the patterns of river stones arranged to form ponds and channels, with water flowing over them, made a great image on long exposure, even on my device.

There was the usual clowning around on the way home, lollies thrown around the bus, stupid songs. People pairing up. We were due back at school after the buses left so parents had been asked to come and pick us up.

Hild and I were still lying with our heads on our bags out front of the school gates at five o'clock. Even the cleaners had gone home.

'She can't have forgotten,' Hild said.

I wasn't so sure. 'Is my face as red as yours?'

'Yup.'

'We were in the shade. With hats on.'

'Reflection off the water, maybe,' Hild said.

We watched a white ute loaded with timber tear down the hill and take the corner too fast.

'Is that your dad?'

We jumped to our feet. Dad pulled up in front of us with a screech.

'Get in,' he said.

I opened the back door, threw in our bags and climbed in after them. It was the observatory work vehicle that Blair usually drove.

'Where's Dianella?' I said. 'Where's our car?'

'Narrabri,' he said. 'Your mother has been arrested.'

'What the fuck?' Hild said.

Dad turned and opened his mouth as if to comment on her language, but shut it again.

'I have to pick up the solicitor from the airport on the way. Do want to come with us, Hild? Or should I drop you home?'

'My parents are away in Canberra,' Hild said.

Dad slapped his forehead. 'Sleepover. That's right. Okay.'

'Why do we need a solicitor?' I said.

'The anti-protester laws. They're refusing to release her on bail.'

'Wait,' Hild said. 'I thought she was on a photoshoot.'

'So did I,' Dad said.

⸻

Dad squinted into the headlights of oncoming traffic on the long straight stretch of road. The dash controls reflected red on the windscreen. Hild was asleep, head against the window, legs across mine in the back of the dual cab. I shifted my feet on the floor in front of me, pushing aside Dianella's camera bag.

'Did she tell you what happened?'

'That group she's working with were protesting against the outsourcing of CSIRO functions to MuX.'

'What do you think?'

'Well, I agree. It's a slippery slope.'

'But ...'

'Well, given who we work for, and my position, it's not a good look.'

A loaded B-triple thundered past, rattling our windows and the pieces of timber on the tray.

'What's all that wood for, anyway?' I said.

'We're building crates, to ship some gear.'

The main telescope is so specialised that they had to design and build components and instruments themselves. Any change, damage or upgrade required onsite solutions. At times, Dad oversaw a team of engineers, electricians, carpenters and robotics specialists. The observatory workshop was equipped with benches, lathes, grinders, saws, welders and high-precision instruments. Every project was unique and everyone in the team multi-skilled. They had to be. Between them, they could probably design and make just about anything.

I turned away from the oncoming headlights. 'The solicitor said they're facing jail time?'

'It's possible,' Dad said.

Hild stretched her legs and opened her eyes. 'What did they do?'

'Rigged up a vertical banner to each of the telescopes. Nelly took pictures, of course, trying to get the core over the top, and uploaded them online. Apparently they disabled company vehicles as well. But Nelly's saying she wasn't part of that. The solicitor thinks she can get her out in the morning. If the security cameras back up her story.'

I reached for my device to open Dianella's profile. But it had already been shut down.

07:20:00

AT LAST, WE SEE a sign for the Narrabri exit. Terry crosses his fingers on both hands. One thousand metres of good luck is all we need. When we reach the turnoff, I drop down to fifty kilometres an hour. Terry relaxes in his seat and slides the goggles back on top of his head.

We rattle over the old wooden bridge, crossing the great Namoi River, flowing wide and brown beneath us, twisting through the town. I turn off the main road, and turn again, until I find the showground. I pull over in the shade of an old river redgum, its gnarled limbs leaning over us, and cut the engine.

We sit for a moment, in the silence, not moving, not vibrating. Then I open the door, swing out my legs and place my boots on firm ground. Terry is already running across the dry grass to the public toilet.

The showground and its surrounds are overflowing with a hotchpotch of old vans, buses, car bodies and tents, amid strings of faded washing and smoking campfires. At first I think them part of the eclipse-mania. But these are residents, not astro-tourists. A group of women works a makeshift garden plot, bent over uneven rows. Sticks and posts hold swathes of mismatching netting above vegetables and salad greens.

A beat-up coffee van mounts the curb and parks on the grass. People appear from behind doors and curtains, drawn by the smell of ground beans. Everyone needs caffeine and there will be a cash economy. A gang of kids set out for the town, probably to scab food or steal items to hock. No one here is going to call the police.

Terry makes his way back, wiping his hands on his T-shirt.

'Are there showers?'

'Yes,' he says.

'We should have a quick clean up while we can,' I say. 'I'll go first. Watch our stuff.'

When I stand, my muscles are stiff and walking seems more difficult than it should. I take my toiletries kit, chamois and clean underwear from my pack, and crunch across the grass. A young woman, no older than me, passes me in the doorway, a new baby strapped to her chest. Something makes me turn to check the child's face. It's a lot like Terry's. I know I shouldn't, but I feel sick.

I hang my things on the hook on the back of the shower cubicle door and use the toilet. The floor is littered with empty vapes, condom wrappers, tiny plastic packets and broken ampules. What I really need is more tampons but the dispenser is credit or coin and all I have is a few crumpled notes.

I take the multi-tool from its case and remove two screws, but the others are rusted shut.

A heli takes off on the other side of town. At the airport, maybe. The noise sets my blood rushing in my ears, my heart pounding. I take hold of the metal cover with both hands and wrench it down.

'Stupid thing!'

On the second try, I get enough leverage to bend the metal. When I reach inside, a sharp edge nicks the inside of my forearm. There are three packets of two left. I take them all, stash them in my pockets, and leave the machine hanging open.

I shut the shower cubicle door and strip off my clothes. The old gas hot water system is coin operated, so it's a cold shower. The shock of it takes my breath. I stand under the stream, washing off the Pilliga, rust-coloured water and blood swirling around my feet and down the hair-clogged drain. When I lean my forehead against the tiles, the sobbing starts, as if it has been sitting there in my throat, just waiting for water.

Everyone stepped up during Dad's last weeks. Blair's broad shoulders filled the doorways, asking what else he could do. Stella was always in the kitchen, washing up while something delicious cooked in the oven, the smells reminding us that we were still hungry, still alive. Even Jade, hanging out in my room, legs crossed, eyes closed, just listening to retro music. And Uncle Nate, turning up outside to take me on another walk, far into the park, keeping my feet moving over the ground, my eyes on the horizon. Trying to teach me to tread lightly, to think like a bird. I'm not sure I even thanked him.

Dad was conscious just before the end. His life, or his work at least, was all about the big questions: how did time begin? And are we alone in the universe? It didn't seem right that he should be so reduced. And yet, the way he stared out the window at the range those last days was just like the way he used to gaze at the light of a distant star. I could see the glow on his face.

The last thing he said was, 'I love you, little bird. Make sure you fly.'

My mother and I were with him when he left. She actually cried in front of me. We cried together. But not for long; there was too much to do.

Stella and Dan helped us wash his body, wrap him in cloth, and carry him out to one of the ATVs. We placed him in the cypress pine box, that Blair had built. He drove us to where the others were waiting – one hand on the wheel, the other on my shoulder. Pete and Uncle Nate had already dug the hole, removing first the leaf litter, then the topsoil, then the rocks and subsoil. We lowered the box and sprinkled woodchips around it, and returned the soil layers to the grave in their original order.

We had a little ceremony there, on the side of Mount Woorut. No suits, no cheesy music, no stuffy church. We were all barefoot.

The Thinning

A male wedge-tailed eagle passed low overhead while Uncle Nate was speaking. It helped to think of Dad's spirit shifting to raptor, but we were left behind, on the ground.

We buried him as the sun went down, and afterwards we sat and sang songs that weren't really sad, and Des played the guitar. Jade didn't say much, probably didn't know what to say, but she only left my side to fetch us more cider.

Dad had wanted to be composted and scattered beneath a grove of ironbarks on the mountain. But even if we could get a message to the Recompose people, there wasn't time for all that. It didn't feel good, not granting his wishes, but we did the best we could.

Dianella and I packed up the next day, although neither of us had really slept. We threw out any food we couldn't carry, emptied the bins, secured the doors and windows, and walked away. It was too soon, too brutal, but it would only have been a matter of time before the police followed up on the report from the hospital and came looking.

Dad's death was just one of many. 'There's no point feeling sorry for ourselves,' Dianella said. 'There are greater losses afoot.'

But he was my *father*, my lodestar.

06:10:00

WE AREN'T THE ONLY ones taking the backroad. It's a shortcut from the Kamilaroi Highway to Kaputar. But we blend in better with the ragtag of camping and recreational vehicles. They've come on motorbikes and bikes, even other ATVs. And they've come on foot: in ones and twos, whole families, laden with lumpy packs and tired, sunburnt faces. Completes and Incompletes, Indigenous and non-Indigenous, all nations, all backgrounds, all ages. And there are more girls and young women among them, the most we've seen so far.

The umbraphiles have always come, like our nosy neighbours back at the tower, who plan and book years ahead. The tour groups of photographers and stargazers, and regular people who happen to live nearby, people bringing their children to see the spectacle. But this is something bigger, new and old at the same time. It's a pilgrimage.

The Nandewar Range comes into view, growing larger as we drive. In profile it resembles what Dianella would call a good histogram: a series of solid peaks in the centre, suggesting a range of mid tones, and nothing off the charts at either end. But I know how steep the climb will be.

Astronomical phenomena have always portended the end of an age, or the birth of a new one. A transformation. And something needs to change, or the end will come anyway – for humans at least.

'How did your parents feel,' I say. 'When they had you?'

'They did the test beforehand, so they knew. And they decided to keep me,' he says.

'I'm glad,' I say. And I find that I am.

'Dad had to look after me when I was little. Take me to appointments. People felt sorry for him, he said. That made him angry.'

'What about feeling sorry for you?'

'Oh, yes. So much pity,' he says. 'There was this one nurse, though. She was nice. More like a friend,' he says.

'She played with you?'

'We did puzzles. And watched movies if I was in hospital overnight. Or played computer games if I had pain.'

The traffic slows and slows again. The fitter walkers are passing the cars now. Many of them are thin, their clothes and shoes worn. A young couple smile at us. There is kindness in them, weariness, too. The word faith comes to mind.

We move forward and then pause, forward and pause. Terry looks at my watch, again. I slap the steering wheel with my hands. 'We don't have time for this!'

When we round the corner, we see the solid line slinking ahead. We're into the campground, vehicles parked in neat lines in the flat brown paddocks either side of the road, like at a festival. Farmers must have opened up their land. For a fee, no doubt.

Crawling along like this, people have too much time to look around. We can hear them talking and laughing, but not what they're saying. Terry is tense, gripping his seat. He switches the Parks beanie for his cap and pulls it down low.

Then the traffic comes to a complete stop.

'Pass me the binoculars?'

Terry opens the glovebox and, after some fumbling, extracts them from their case. I have to stop myself from snatching them out of his hands.

Police and Parks have set up a boom gate at the entrance. Some vehicles are being turned around or directed into a cordoned-off area where there are more police waiting.

'There's a checkpoint,' I say.

I home in on anyone in Parks uniforms, hoping against hope to recognise one of the staff, or find some flaw or work-around. A hole in the fence. Anything to get through to the other side. Dianella says there is always a way in; you just have to find it. They're searching the vehicle at the head of the line, and the driver, using a portable reader to scan her wrist.

In an instant, it shifts from smiles to her out of the car, hands on the back of her head, legs spread, pushed down over the bonnet. I lower the binoculars.

'They're scanning chips on entry,' I say.

Tension is rising around us, too. People are muttering, looking at their devices, sending messages. Some are getting out of their cars, abandoning them by the side of the road and continuing on foot.

Over the fence, the campground is a sea of vans and tents, or utes and cars with just an annex over a tarp. There are queues for the toilets and queues for the food stalls. People gathered around fires, people roaming around looking at the spectacle, people setting up telescopes, street photographers capturing the scenes.

It's chaos. And that's going to help us.

I check my watch: five hours, forty minutes. We can still walk to the top in that time.

The line starts moving again. But I pull off the road and park the ATV on the verge.

'Fin?'

'Take everything from the front,' I say.

Terry empties the glovebox into his bag. I leap out, smiling at the family behind us with two young daughters, maybe twins, as I grab my pack. As if all this is completely normal. Terry is out, slinging his pack over his shoulders. At the last minute, I run back, lean in and take the keys from the ignition.

'In case we need it later,' I say, as though Terry had asked a question.

He startles when I put my arm over his shoulder. 'Walk fast, act confident,' I say.

We wade through long grass, old cans, bottles and plastic packets, towards the fence. Someone shouts but we do not turn or hesitate. I hold the wires apart for Terry and follow him through, into the campground.

05:34:00

IT'S THE BIGGEST CROWD I've seen gathered together since the protests. On the surface, it's a festival atmosphere: music and smoky fires, colourful clothes and beanies, dreadlocks and shaved heads. Someone is handing out temporary sun tattoos, and a nearby stall is selling T-shirts and singlets printed with 'The Sun is our One True God'. It's true enough; our day star gave us life.

There is a long line for a face-painting kiosk. The most popular design seems to be all white with a black star over one eye, or what looks like a spray of stars on one cheek. There are less young women than men, but more than we've been seeing. More than I would have expected.

Quite a few families have Incomplete children, though most are younger than Terry.

'Did you get the voice recorder?'

'It's in the top of my pack,' he says.

I unzip the pocket and pull it out. 'So many people. All different sorts. People you wouldn't normally see together. Bright colours, constant movement, noise. Laughing. The vibe is anticipation, excitement, but there is something else.'

In space, things are not always as they appear. Like Mars, who looks hot but is actually a cold planet now. And Venus, who looks icy cold but is actually hellish hot. She was much like Earth once, but now Venus's surface is the hottest in the solar system, bar the sun.

'We're here to witness a cosmic event, something bigger than any of us. But within the chaos, there are patterns. Something else is happening, something planned and organised below the surface. People are communicating with each other, making eye contact or just giving a nod. Mostly younger people, but they have allies. People my mother's age, Indigenous and non-Indigenous. There are a lot of other Illegals in here –'

'How can you tell?' Terry says.

I stop the recorder. 'They're not carrying devices,' I say.

The dark purple flags are fluttering everywhere. Up close, we see that the symbol is a rainbow spiral. It could be DNA or the Milky Way. It's on T-shirts and caps, and that's what the cheek patterns are, too.

A line of uniformed police is walking through the crowd, coming in our direction. Illegals scatter ahead of them. I choose a family to follow, and am about to step after them when a hand grips my shoulder. I freeze, torn between pushing Terry away and holding him tighter.

'Fin?'

When I turn, it's really her. Thinner, her head shaved. But it's her.

'Hild!'

She half-smiles and only for a moment. 'Don't go that way,' she says. 'Come with me.'

She spins me around and drags me by the hand, weaving and dodging through the crowd. Now I see it in young peoples' faces. They're not here for mindless fun or spectacle; they have purpose. I hang on tight to Hild and Terry hangs on tight to my pack. She stops on the other side of the queue for a juice vendor.

We stand there, hugging each other, a still point amid all the noise and movement. Relief floods my body. And so many other overwhelming emotions that I can't separate.

She releases first. 'I recognised your walk a mile off.'

'And I knew your voice.' I'm sniffing back tears. It's so long since I felt joy that it hurts. We're the same people but adults now, and that hurts, too.

'One question,' she says. 'What the hell are you doing here? And why are you covered in dirt?'

'That's two questions.' I brush dust from my sleeves. 'We're here for the eclipse.'

'But ... it's not safe.' She looks Terry up and down.

'Hild, this is Terry.'

'Hello, Hild,' he says.

'Hey,' she says, with more questions behind her high eyebrows.

'It's a long story,' I say. 'You're here with your parents?'

'Just Dad. He bought a flash telescope for the occasion. Mel's here, too.'

Hild's little sister would be a teenager now. Cute, and a talented musician, but one of those non-stop talkers, always wanting to tag along when we wanted to be alone.

Hild stares at Terry a little too long. 'Sorry,' she says. 'But your face. It's all over the socials.'

'Are you sure?' Terry says. 'People say we all look the same.'

Hild blinks. 'It's definitely you. They're saying your parents are spies. And that you're ... a person of interest. The cap and glasses help but –'

'Who's saying that?' I say. 'His parents were kidnapped. And they were hunting him.'

She holds up her hands. 'That's just what I'm seeing online.'

Someone from the queue turns to stare.

Hild touches her finger to her lips. 'Camp with us?' she says. 'You'd be safer. And we can talk more.'

'We need to be up top,' I say.

'You're setting up for Dianella?'

I nod.

Terry opens his mouth to speak but when I cough, he gets it and shuts up.

'How is Nelly?'

'She's ... harder than she was.'

Hild nods but there is something knowing in her expression, the way she's holding her mouth.

My stomach flip-flops.

'There's a shuttle up to the information bay every thirty minutes,' Hild says.

'We'll never get through,' I say. 'They're scanning chips.'

'I might be able to get you on,' she says. 'I'll book it now.' She pulls up an app and taps on the screen of her device.

'Won't they still scan us?' Terry says.

'Not if I go with you,' she says. 'It's vomit-worthy but there are privileges for those of us who are in the system.' She adds a child ticket to the two adults.

I search Hild's face for bitterness. 'What was it like?'

'In the beginning, it was just testing. Like they said. But those of us who are lucky enough to be class one fertile were called back to donate eggs. That was gross enough. Lined up like battery hens, waiting to be harvested. And the procedure ... It's not pleasant.'

I flinch, an all-body reaction. 'You said in the beginning ...'

'Now they want more. Of course.'

'More eggs?'

'It turns out that lab fertilisations have a low success rate.' Hild stares out into the crowd. 'They're monitoring my cycle. If it all lines up with the donor, I'll have to go in for impregnation at some point.'

'You're not serious?' Just the word is sickening.

'Oh, I'm serious.'

'Fuck's sake,' I say. 'It's like women have lost control of their bodies all over again.'

'I don't think we ever really had it,' Hild says. Her face is so calm. Too calm.

'Do you know who he is?'

Hild's eyes rest on Terry for a moment. 'First generation. A family with a lot of money, evidently.'

'Don't do it,' I say. 'Run. Come with us.'

She holds out her wrist.

I trace my fingers over the bump beneath the skin. The microchip that not only monitors her cycle, but her every movement. I have to swallow to stop myself being sick. 'When did they do this?'

'When I first went in for testing.'

It's all turned out just like Dianella said. 'I'm sorry I wasn't there with you.'

She shakes her head. 'I'm glad you got away. I wasn't there for you when your dad died, either.'

'You heard?'

'Of course we did,' she says. 'At least he was able to be at home.'

'That wasn't easy,' I say.

'I'm sure it wasn't.'

I can feel Terry looking at me. All the colours around us have blurred into purple, swirling in my peripheral vision.

'How long do you have?' I say.

'A couple of months,' she says. 'Maybe six.'

I'm shaking my head. 'They can't *make* you be pregnant.'

'You don't understand. It's like conscription. They say we're doing our bit for the survival of the human race.'

'There must be *something* we can do, Hild.'

'Yeah.' She makes proper eye contact for the first time. 'I'm not letting Mel go through it. Put it that way.'

'What about your parents?'

'Dad wants to pull the pin. But they gave Mum a promotion, and she went back to the capital. Now we're not sure we can even trust her. They're probably separating. It's a fucking shitshow, babes.'

'I'm sorry,' I say. I want to be strong but tears are pouring out. This isn't how it was meant to be.

'Please don't cry,' Hild says. 'You know it sets me off.'

'You can remove the chip,' Terry says. He rubs the spot on his arm.

Hild nods but looks over his head, into the crowd again. 'C'mon,' she says. 'We have to catch this bus. And you need to get out of those uniforms. That's not going to fool anyone. There are actual Parks staff everywhere. You look like a couple of kids playing dress-ups.'

I open my mouth to object. I'm older than Hild, for a start. But we follow her to the line of portable composting toilets. Hild waits off to one side, tapping the screen of her device.

I change into my own clothes, elbows smacking the walls of the cubicle. I stash the Parks gear – except the beanie – in the bin, beneath used bamboo towelling. Then I wash my face with the trickle of tepid water and rub in moisturiser, run my hands through my hair and tie it up. My cheeks are red from windburn but I'm a little more presentable. And different to when we arrived, which feels important.

Terry is out before me. His hair is neat again, free of dust and styled in the front. He waits so that we can walk back side by side.

'What did you do with the clothes?' I say.

'In the bottom of the bin,' he says. 'I kept the beanie though.'

'Good job.'

Hild slips her device into her jeans pocket and looks us up and down. 'Better. Let's go.'

We follow her along the back of the food and drink stalls. I inhale mango and ginger, yeast and cinnamon, something frying in cardamom – and coffee. My mouth waters. Not just from hunger but a craving for flavour and texture. Something that doesn't contain goat or oats. A piccolo in a little ceramic cup.

Hild removes her sunglasses. 'Borrow these, Terry. Your eyes are the biggest give-away.'

'I won't be able to see.' He clenches his fists in front of him.

'That shouldn't matter on the bus. Walk between Finley and me, and keep your head down. We'll just have to hope everyone's focused on the eclipse.'

'Most people look away anyway,' Terry says.

I can't read Terry's face, or his tone, but he tucks in between us, hanging onto my pack. We arrive at the back of the queue as the shuttle pulls up, almost noiseless. Terry stands close while Hild steps forward and displays her screen. I hold my breath while the driver scans the tickets and then Hild's wrist, without even glancing at us, and we follow her up the steps.

In the end, it's that easy.

04:59:00

I TAKE THE WINDOW seat second from the back and Terry slides in next to me. Hild sits in front of us, like a shield. We pile our packs next to her. The seats fill and then the aisle. It's uncomfortable being pressed in but fewer people have a clear view of us, which isn't a bad thing. I have a thousand questions, most of which I can't ask in such a close space.

'How was the rest of school?' I say.

'Well, there were seventeen girls and thirty-nine boys. So that was kind of nuts. Frankie and the other non-binary peeps never came back.'

I shake my head. Frankie was the heart of our year, running the school magazine and the social club, organising fundraisers and events.

'It was hard,' Hild says. 'People you've known all your life just disappearing. But we bonded, you know. Elsa came first.'

It's not right, but I'm jealous, of all I missed out on. 'No surprises there,' I say. 'And you?'

Hild smiles. 'Second. In your absence.'

'That's great,' I say. 'Uni?'

'I got my first choices. Melbourne and UQ. But I had to defer,' she says. 'With all this. They'll hold my position indefinitely. And waive the fees if I … comply.'

My stomach is roiling. 'What would you study?'

'Genetics, maybe.'

'Whoa. I did not see that coming.'

'I'm thinking animals and plants, not humans. If it happens.'

'What about Ms Lander?' I say.

'She never came back,' Hild said. 'We were told she resigned but …'

'She was so brave.'

'She has two girls of her own. She totally got it.'

'And we called her cold.'

'I know,' Hild said. 'We got a lot of things wrong.'

Terry is fidgeting, touching his glasses in his shirt pocket. He's not the only Incomplete on the bus, but the others are with their parents. The family in front of us has an older regular daughter and an Incomplete, a girl, I think. People are either staring or making a point of not staring. It's the similarities and differences between them, the idea of the mix. And the mixed feelings the parents might have.

The spent paddocks and tree-lined driveways peter out and we're returned to forest. The shuttle lurches through a series of potholes and loose bitumen. The woman in front of Hild grips the back of her seat to steady herself. I had assumed that all the purple wristbands were for ticketholders, but they feature the same spiral helix as the flags, hats and T-shirts.

'Seen Jade?' Hild says.

'Day before yesterday,' I say.

'She with anyone?'

'Seriously? We only see each other. And not that often.'

'I'm kidding,' she says.

I smile and shake my head. She's still Hild underneath. There is something dark on her left arm, poking out from under her shirt. When I reach for it over the seat, she pulls her sleeve down and puts her hand on mine.

'Did you hear about *Voyager*?'

'What?'

'It's talking. Sending data. It's woken up and started shooting back weird messages.'

'*Voyager II*?'

'No. The first one. There are teams all over the world trying to figure it out. Decryption experts, astronomers. Your Dad would have loved it.'

'When was this?'

'Maybe a week ago.'

She leaves her hand on mine and I splay my fingers to intertwine with hers. The bus climbs into a hairpin bend. Nandewar's knobbly peaks and crags loom above us. And then a glimpse of Kaputar herself, shrouded in mist.

The bus slows, edging through the crowd gathered around

the parking bay. There are not as many people as at base camp but they're more closely packed, and the atmosphere more intense. I can almost hear the energy crackling.

The driver pulls up next to the Parks information sign. *We're in.* But now I'm going to have to say goodbye to Hild all over again.

Our fellow passengers slip into their backpacks and grab their water bottles. Hild squeezes my fingers and releases my hand. She stands and heads down the aisle. We go to follow but the people in the back seat push in front, separating us from her. The driver watches us all the way down the aisle in his mirror.

'Thanks,' I say, smiling and raising my hand. Dianella taught me to bluff and smile, even if people are hostile towards you. Especially if they are hostile towards you. I feel into my memories of her, trying to sense if she's close. But no images come. Just a sudden downward pitch in my stomach, as if something big and maybe bad is about to happen.

Terry clutches my pack as we navigate the bus steps. The fugitive, as they're calling him. Just a kid who is scared of everything. And then we're out, back in fresh air. I suck in three big lungfuls.

We pass the line of people waiting to go back to base camp. Press, podcasters and volunteers not staying on the mountain for the spectacle itself. I position myself between them and Terry, putting my arm over his shoulder until we reach Hild, who is waiting by a stand of young ironbarks.

Everything is movement: people adjusting their boots, zipping up packs, setting out for the summit. My nose twitches at the concentration of laundry detergent, hair product, sunscreen, deodorant, perfume, insect repellent and pheromones.

Again, some people seem to have a separate purpose, more watchful and aware. A Koori woman turns from her circle and smiles, reminding me of Uncle Nate's parting words. I smile but drop my eyes. I'm not sure enough to trust. Or to impose myself.

'So, babes,' Hild says. 'Keep to yourselves. There will be a lot of press live-streaming from up on the summit. So keep your faces out of that, obviously.'

'Thank you,' I say. I was determined not to cry but the tears are coming anyway.

Terry hands back Hild's sunglasses and slides on his glasses. He blinks, focuses, and settles.

'Take care, Terry,' Hild says, without looking at him.

I get it. But he notices. There's that little fall on his face. Everyone wants Hild to like them.

'Do give my love to Nelly,' she says.

'Uh-huh.' There is something in her tone but I'm too busy trying to keep myself together.

'Find us afterwards?'

'Sure.' I take in the untidy sea of people, weighing the feeling in my stomach, wondering if there will even be an afterwards.

'We're in the yellow camper, on the high point.'

'Got it.'

'I'd better go.' She looks back towards the bus, the last few people piling on.

'Hild?'

She turns, and with the light on her face, I see how much she has changed. Has been changed. The way she holds herself, the worry lines on her forehead. There is already so much I don't know.

'I love you,' I say.

Her smile transforms her face back into the one I know, and she's beautiful.

'I love you, too, Finley Kelvin. See you on the other side.'

ASTRONOMICAL TWILIGHT

Mount Kaputar National Park

Gamilaraay Country

04:38:00

WE START WALKING, UP the road, up the mountain, just two people in the crowd. Most are focused on the climb, each other, and the anticipation of what lies ahead, but some do take a second look at Terry. There are fewer Illegals on this side of the checkpoint and more of the rebirthing mob, reeking of incense and essential oils. I focus on the wattle and cypress pines closing in around us, the sense of leaving the plain and joining the mountains.

'Why did you lie?' Terry says.

'What?'

'To Hild.' He forces his words out between puffs. 'About why we are here.'

'I didn't lie,' I say. 'I just didn't tell her everything. Dianella told me not to tell anyone.'

'But you're closer to Hild.'

'In a way,' I say. 'But this is bigger, I think.'

'Do you trust her?'

'Hild would never betray us,' I say. 'If that's what you mean.'

Terry shakes his head. 'Why don't you trust her one hundred percent?'

'Eighteen months is a long time. She's been through things I don't understand. Has different motivations now.'

'But what she said about her little sister ... And I think she knew we weren't meeting your mother.'

'You're saying we should've told her?'

Terry nods.

My throat constricts. 'Well, it's done now.'

'Was she your girlfriend? Before.'

'No!'

He watches me loosen the watch strap on my wrist and tighten it again. The plastic is so uncomfortable, always sweaty underneath.

'Stop it. Get out of my head.'

'Sorry,' he says. 'It's just your thoughts are –'

'She's my best friend.' And now I'm crying again.

Terry is still watching me, his bug eyes all glassy.

'What? Why are *you* crying?'

He shakes his head.

'Does everyone just accept all this procreation crap?'

'No,' Terry says. 'The right argue that it is a duty, like Hild said. But the left say women and girls should not be forced. There are privacy concerns. The non-binary community objects. And the environmental movement argues that we should allow our population to decline, to reduce pressure on the planet.'

'Well, that makes sense, at least.'

'Even if it means we die out?'

'Maybe.'

The mountains loom over us, ramparts shrouded in mist. The sight pulls me up. Kaputar's summit is a ceremonial place and people are swarming all over.

'Wait a sec,' I say.

Kaputar, Nandewar. I am Fin. We have travelled from the Warrumbungles and the Pilliga. We're climbing without permission, with no elder to guide us. We are here to witness the eclipse, to be part of ... whatever change is coming. We know you hold all the stories of the past. And as we live this one out, please lead us on.

Terry is staring at what he thinks is the peak. 'We're walking up *that*? How high is it?'

'Fifteen hundred metres,' I say. 'They nearly put the observatory up there, actually. The community spent years building a road. This road, I guess. But in the end, they chose Siding Spring instead.'

I'm still waiting for some kind of sign from the mountain but with so many people around, I can't get a read on whether we're moving with or against the flow. And it's not like we can turn around. We'll just have to trust and accept the consequences.

The solicitor couldn't get Dianella out of lockup until the Monday. When I got home from school, she was sitting at the kitchen table in front of her device, piles of paper around her and all over the floor. She looked tired and worn, like someone else's mother. I stopped in the doorway.

'Hey, Finley.'

'You okay?' I said.

'Hanging out for a good night's sleep in my own bed. Sorry to worry you.'

'What happens now?'

She gestured at the paperwork. 'We fight the charges. The hearing isn't for a few weeks. How was Brewarrina?'

'Fair bit of water in the river. A few fish even. People totally got how the traps work.'

Dianella nodded. 'Did you get burnt? Your nose is pink.'

'I had my hat on, cream.'

'It was a stinker, wasn't it. And Hild?'

'In fine form. She … was a good support person over the weekend.'

'I'm glad she was here.'

We had helped Dad and Blair unload the timber from the ute and stack it outside the workshop. Which is when Dad spotted red cloth scraps in the bin. They had made the protest banners inside the main telescope. Dad was in town when it was happening, so someone else had let them in.

Blair admitted it straight away. 'I should have told you, Phil,' he said.

Dad was as mad as I'd ever seen him. 'Told me? You shouldn't have *done* it. What were you thinking?'

They had used university premises, tools, and materials to do something illegal. And Dianella had used deep black optical paint purchased on Dad's work credit card. It was super-specialised, expensive, and traceable by batch number. We were all sweating on the questions that might come up if the case went to trial.

Dad came in the back door carrying a wooden box loaded with vegetables. I stepped aside to let him in.

'From Stella and Dan,' he said.

'That's nice of them,' Dianella said.

Dad nodded but didn't look at her. 'How was school?'

I shrugged. 'Fine.' I couldn't remember a single detail of the day, except my modern history textbook feeling heavy and irrelevant.

'Thought I'd do something with that backstrap for dinner,' Dad said. 'And all these vegetables. Roast them, maybe.'

'Can I help?' Dianella said.

Dad kept his eyes on the carrots he was rinsing beneath the tap. 'Maybe you could clear the table. Make some space.'

'I'll do that, then,' she said.

I backed out of the kitchen and went to my room.

04:15:00

THE MOUNTAIN ISN'T HOME the way the Warrumbungles are, but I know Kaputar. While Dad was alive, we clambered over the Nandewar Range in all four seasons, stayed at all the campgrounds and did every walk on the map. And a few that weren't on it anymore, to waterfalls and deep blue pools worn in the rock over millennia. Where the water is so cold your body goes into shock after diving in. The euphoria afterwards was like nothing else.

We stayed in the huts up top when it snowed one winter holiday, where my parents had their honeymoon, or post-elopement, when it still snowed sometimes in spring. It became their tradition to return every anniversary. They liked to climb up to the Governor, with its three-hundred-and-sixty-degree view, and watch the sunset with a champagne picnic. That's where they decided to have me, in 'a moment of golden hour, bubble-fuelled optimism,' Dianella says. Which is way too much information. I never asked if they regretted bringing me into this world. It kind of goes without saying.

Even at Terry's pace, we're passing people on the climb. People not used to walking, let alone with full packs. There are way more tents being carried in than there are campsites. Parks must be making allowances or have issued special permits. Or maybe they've lost control of the whole thing.

'So steep,' Terry says. His in-breaths are laboured – and loud. For the moment, we have a little space around us.

'Can I ask you a question?' I say.

'Yes,' Terry says.

'Promise to tell the truth?'

He turns to face me. 'Yes.'

'Are your parents spies?'

'I don't think so,' he says. 'If we were living a double life, it was about preparing to disappear. To protect me.'

'You didn't pick up any ... images?'

'Nothing,' Terry says.

'Were they both happy to go? Leave their lives behind.'

'Maybe not happy. But a decision they made together.'

'What's your mother like?'

'Smart, and mostly thinking of bigger things. A bit like yours,' he says. 'But she read to me every night. Even when she was away, she'd take the book with her and call or leave a voicey.'

'Favourite?'

'You'll laugh,' he says.

'Tell me anyway.'

'*The Little Prince.*'

'I love that book,' I say.

'If I could just hear Mum's voice again …'

I close my eyes. 'At least we know they're alive. In the system.'

'Yes.'

03:49:00

THE ROAD LOOPS AND turns back on itself, easing the gradient but lengthening our journey. The broken bitumen is hard underfoot. I can feel hot spots developing on my right toe and left heel. The lower lookouts are already crowded with telescopes and cameras, ranging from high-end professional kit to budget. These people must have hiked in days ago, sleeping on the ground next to their gear.

I don't know whether it's the mountain or the approaching eclipse, but a darkness is settling in. I can't keep seeing all these cameras and not think of Dianella. And when I think of her, it's the image she left the world of herself, on that awful balcony at the too bright edge of what used to be a country town.

We pause to catch our breath, drink, and look out over Mount Ningadhun. I remove my shoes and socks, and take two plasters from the first-aid kit.

'How are those boots?' I say. 'Got any sore spots?' I say. 'You don't want blisters making you miserable.'

'My heels, maybe.'

'Show me.'

He undoes the laces and removes the boots and his thin socks. His feet are so white they glow, except for an angry red patch running down his Achilles.

'Oh yeah,' I say. 'Just in time.'

I stick gel pads on his heels and cover them with waterproof plaster. 'There you go.'

'Thanks,' he says. He's tougher than I thought; they must have been sore.

Ningadhun's vertical walls rise out of the forest, like a weathered medieval fortress, rather than a volcanic plug that cooled millions of years ago after millions of years of fire and rage. Geology is like space, putting our puny lives in perspective.

A group has set up camp on a high point, surrounded by a pit of dense vegetation.

'How did they get up there?' Terry says.

'Ropes,' I say. 'Serious rock climbers.'

Terry finally finishes relacing his boots and we trudge on. I'm starting to count the kilometres and watch the minutes ticking by.

The security cameras at the array had been disabled. But Dianella's solicitor argued that she hadn't damaged any property and couldn't have rigged the ropes to hang the protest banners, or climbed them, as she had photographs of all stages of the process from down on the ground. The government solicitor clearly didn't understand the self-timer function, which had been a feature on digital cameras for two decades – or chose not to. And no one even noticed or tested the paint. We had all worried for nothing.

'Policing isn't what it used to be,' the solicitor said. 'You've been watching too many of those old detective series.'

Dianella got six months good behaviour with community service, which she spent planting trees along the roadsides. The others spent three months in prison.

She was never going to be well-behaved. Not after that. The maps and equipment built up in her studio. There were more meetings with Des and Blair. But she and Dad stopped talking about it in front of me, and the kitchen table was always cleared of whatever operation was in progress by the time I got home.

Dad insisted that I was no longer to be a part of any photoshoots, which stung at first, but left me free to swim in my own lane.

03:27:00

WE CLIMB OUT OF another bend to the sound of raised voices. We're at Green Camp, which means five kilometres done. An argument has broken out. Over who was there first, it seems. An older woman with a neat grey bob speaks up, trying to be reasonable. The men manage to push her out of the way without quite touching her. There is room enough for everyone but both families want the prime spot, in the middle. People are already filming the spectacle. We hang back, waiting for it to break or clear. It isn't something we need to get caught up in, and we definitely don't want to be in anyone's picture gallery.

A willy wagtail lands on the road, hopping short distances, and flicking his tail from side to side, like a black and white flag.

'Hey,' I say.

The men are of similar height and weight but while one has a full head of hair and a beard, the other is shiny bald and clean-shaven. They put down their packs so they can stick their chests out more effectively. I can smell the testosterone and adrenaline, the need to break the tension as the eclipse approaches. The pull of gravity on all of us.

The Thinning

'This is not good,' Terry says.

We try to edge around the circle while everyone is distracted. I'm scanning everything and everyone in every direction, trying to anticipate threats. We just need to get past. And then a teenager in bright white shoes spots Terry and grabs his brother's sleeve.

'Check out the mutant!' he says.

The man with the beard throws a punch. It doesn't land properly but it's enough to snap baldy's head back and now the fight is on. They're flailing all over the road, and the crowd that has gathered has to pull back. Every second person is filming. What a shitshow, Hild would say.

'Let's go off-road for a bit,' I say. 'Keep your head down.'

To cross the clearing and head up the track towards Yulludunida Crater, we have to go right past the brothers. I wait until they're engrossed in the fight but one of them grabs Terry by the sleeve, spinning him around. 'Where do you think you're going, mute?'

Terry falls, flat on his back. The shock sends his glasses flying but his pack stops his head from hitting the bitumen.

'Back off, fatso,' I say.

One of the men turns. 'Hey, you can't say that to my kid.'

'He just called my brother a mutant,' I say.

It's ridiculous. Nothing about us is alike but it shuts them up. The fight has been forgotten. Everyone is looking at us instead. *Perfect.*

I retrieve Terry's glasses, wipe them on my shirt, and help him to his feet. The boy's mother rushes up to put her arms around the bully, as if he's the one who needs protecting. Another man in a cap holds up his device, framing a picture. I step between him and Terry and turn my back.

'Do you two have permits?' the bully's mother says.

'We went through all the same checkpoints as you. This is a national park. We have every right to be here.'

There is a hesitation, people shuffling and uncertain. Anger lingers but no one is sure what to do with it.

'You won't mind showing us your permits, then?' the woman says.

'Oh, for fuck's sake.' I want to punch her smug face. Her kid, too. He's not so much fat as soft, which I have zero tolerance for. The watch on my wrist is counting down the minutes to what might be the biggest event of our lives and these idiots are standing in our way.

Terry leans on me, his body rigid. A vehicle is coming up the road behind us, which can only be Parks or police.

'C'mon.' I grab Terry's arm and push past the woman. We hurry away from the road, onto the walking track.

'Yeah, that's it. Fuck off, freak,' the boy yells after us.

'Kaylan,' his mother says.

'Ignore them,' I say.

'Easy for you to say. You're not the freak.'

It's debatable, but not the point. We climb on, zigzagging through box woodland. The company of trees is an improvement on a crowd of stupid people. At the top of the rise, I stop to get my breath and wait for Terry.

A flame robin calls from a dead branch below me. The view back over the lower range is stunning, but we've got so much further to climb.

Terry stops, hands on his thighs, sucking in mouthfuls of air. His top lip is sweaty. And I see now the hairs trying to grow there, the hint of adult in him.

'Listen,' I say. 'People are pathetic with anyone different.'

'Everyone hates me because of what has happened. The Population Bill. Like Hild.'

'She doesn't hate you,' I say. 'She was kind.'

He nods but his mouth is miserable. 'She helped us.'

'Wait,' I say. 'Tell me you can't see everyone's thoughts about you?'

'Not everyone,' he says. 'But enough.'

'Oh god.' Including mine. Definitely mine. 'I'm so sorry.'

His head drops, but I see his tears.

'Other animals are adapting. And we don't think of them as freaks. What about those birds, the condors, who just started reproducing asexually. And the stingrays, pregnant without any males, in that tank in Queensland. Fish, frogs, reptiles – they're all transforming.' They probably aren't the best comparisons – being so far from human.

Terry nods. 'But with us ... They're saying it was a virus now.'

'That's how we got most of our adaptations. Like the uterus.'

He pulls a face, like he might vomit.

'However it happened, you and I aren't that different. We came from different environments, but we've ended up in the same place.'

The corners of his mouth turn up. Just a little.

'C'mon, we can get ahead of those clowns.'

I follow a goat track heading directly uphill.

'Do you know where you're going?' Terry says.

'*Yes*,' I say.

03:03:00

WE FOLLOW THE CREEK until the trees thin and the slope steepens. We've reached the grasstree line. They're gathered in spiky stands, hair billowing in the breeze. I feel stronger for their presence, a connection to the park at home.

'Hey,' I say. 'I'm back.'

We step through the old dingo fence, and I push the pace, shutting out Terry's wheezing behind me. I'm not sure if we can even get to the top in time, let alone find a good position. Not without fighting someone for it. The path is steep and rough, barely a path. Only good for goats. I stop to strip down to my T-shirt, my back and chest sweaty.

The little bluebells are out in their thousands, and I notice for the first time that when they are fully open, in sun, their five petals form a perfect star. I'll take it as a sign that we're on the right track.

When I stop to look out across the knobbly crater, maybe it's just the wind across the rock, but it's calling me. It's not really a crater at all but an old ring-dyke, where an underground pool of molten rock drained away and the roof collapsed. The remaining ridge would be a great spot to watch the eclipse, and make a good image, with the crater and grasstrees in the foreground. Only a handful of people have braved the climb so far.

A wedge-tailed eagle soars along the spine, hunting the small mammals who are out hunting for people's crumbs. I imagine the exact curve of her bill, her amber eyes, the rufous streaks on her nape. Then I lose focus; the horizon spins, my blood rushes in my ears. When I see again, it's with binocular vision: the twitching whiskers and dark tail tip of an antechinus from above. And yet, one eye is on the sky, with a whole other dimension of colour, and the centreline of the Earth's gravitation field steadying me. I hold the wind with my primary feathers for a moment, and *swoop*, talons outstretched ...

And then I'm back on the ground in heavy boots, one-dimensional and breathless, watching the eagle rise, with her catch in one claw. I turn, looking for Terry, but he's still struggling up the slope behind me.

What was that?

Terry flops down on a rock, red in the face. He gulps down a great lot of water, spilling it over his shirt, and takes his eyedrops from his pocket.

'What were you doing down at the spring that morning anyway?' I say.

'I heard water running and wanted to see. I didn't know there would be anyone there.'

'Did you get a good look?'

His face turns even redder. 'I didn't mean to,' he says. 'And you know my eyes aren't good.'

'Uh-huh,' I say. I also know that he saw me well enough to recognise my face when I found him hiding.

'My parents were fighting,' he says. 'I didn't want to be inside anymore.'

'What about?'

'Dad wanted to finish the job first. Mum wanted to go that morning.'

'She had a bad feeling?'

'Yes,' he says. 'Did your parents argue?'

'Not really,' I say.

Dad did get an opportunity to build on his research. NASA asked him to come back on contract for their Origin Stars project. The catch was, Dianella and I couldn't go. It was the only time I ever saw my mother lose her shit. There were no secrets in that house; it was small and the walls were thin.

'Who is going to raise our child?' Dianella said.

'You can both visit,' he said. 'It's only eighteen months.'

'We both know how those things drag out.'

'Two years, max. The end date is in the contract.'

'Why even ask me then? You've made up your mind.'

Dad removed his glasses and rubbed his eyes. 'I thought we were having a conversation, Nelly.'

'But you want this.'

'I need this. My career needs this. It's a second chance.'

Dianella shakes her head. 'I don't even know who you are anymore.'

'What's that supposed to mean?'

'I thought our project was staying here and fighting for what we believe in?'

'I'm tired of fighting, Nelly.' He covered his face with his hands. 'In fire-affected areas, they have no choice but to phase out mobile towers. It's pointless rebuilding them. And some of these satellites, that's how we get our data. How the observatory functions. It's more complicated than you like to think.'

'It's only as complicated as we make it,' Dianella said.

My mother was not tired of fighting. There was a Kelvin standoff. I stayed out of it, though I didn't want Dad leaving the country any more than she did.

Dad asked NASA for more time to make a decision. Then travel restrictions delayed the start date. Priorities in space exploration shifted to resources, and he never ended up going. I wonder if he regretted that. Or if my mother regretted opposing it. What discoveries he might have made – if any of them might have made a difference.

02:18:00

I KEEP MOUNT CORYAH on my right until I find the track that leads us back to the road. At last, we're up on the plateau. The detour has saved us time and kept us safe, but we're still racing the clock. Terry, to be fair, is being a little trooper. He hasn't complained once, though his hands are scratched and bleeding.

The higher we go, the more young women we see. More Illegals, too. They must have walked in ahead of the blockade, on the backtrails. Before Parks staff were patrolling. Or maybe they're turning a blind eye.

A mist is moving in, some sort of cold front. The mountain always has had its own weather. It can be eight degrees cooler at the summit than down on the plains. We stop to shove down chocolate-espresso powerbars, which I've saved for last.

Terry flexes his left bicep and presses it with his finger as he chews.

'Bulking up?'

He smiles. 'Maybe.'

'It's from hanging onto that roll bar. In the ATV.'

'Your driving, you mean.'

'Ha.'

I crumple my power-bar wrapper into a tiny ball and tuck it into the hip pocket of my pack. My body temperature has dropped in the cool and Terry's arms are goosebumped. We take our fleeces and beanies from our packs and put them on.

'Those experiments,' I say. 'Did they hurt you?'

'Not really. It's just being hooked up to a lot of monitors. I do not like them touching my eyes though.'

'That's uncomfortable?'

'Yes,' he says. 'And … if I hadn't been so young, at the start, I would have known to keep more to myself.'

'About your powers?'

He almost smiles. 'My superpowers, yes.'

I start walking and Terry follows. 'Did they find out how you read minds?'

'I could never do it in the lab. Too much pressure.'

'How did they know, then?'

'My parents told them,' he says.

'Seriously?' I shake my head. 'Kids should raise themselves now. Adults aren't fit.'

'Maybe,' he says.

'It's not their fault. The world just changed too fast.'

☾

The higher we climb, the more congested the lookouts. Parks staff are struggling to keep people inside the taped-off areas at

Bark Hut campground. Someone has lit a fire. There are way too many people. Everyone wants their premium eclipse experience.

At the Governor carpark, I watch a woman attaching her device to a telescope. There are so many tripods and cameras tangled in close proximity, it's an accident waiting to happen. Dianella couldn't have stood it.

I imagine her walking straight past the lookout, carting all her gear along the boardwalk, up to the rocky zigzag track and ladders to the old throat of the volcano. The edge is so exposed, it would be easy to drop a lens cap or battery, even one of her precious lenses. But Dianella was so methodical, she never did. Not in front of me, anyway. It was hard work growing up around someone who never made mistakes.

We would have had to be up on Governor days ahead to stake out the best spot. A week, maybe, eating dehydrated goat and shitting in tubes. Still, that would be better than imagining the danger Dianella is placing herself in this time.

I check the numbers on my watch and up the pace. Only one thing is certain: the eclipse is coming. And nothing can stop it. There is something liberating about giving ourselves over to the workings of the universe. To the currents moving underground, between the roots of trees, talking to stones, shifting deep within the rock.

Everything is unravelling on this mountain.

02:10:00

THE ROAD LEVELS OUT into open forest, through glistening trunks: snow, ribbon and mountain gums. The understory is all silver wattle and blackwood on a carpet of snow grass. It's another shift, the air crisp and sharp, sub-alpine. The higher we go, the more we leave the world behind. Small birds call and currawongs work the canopy. The worst of the climb is over but it's still another four or five kilometres until we reach the trailhead.

'Fin!'

'What?'

'What is this?'

Something makes me turn. Some memory of my own wonder, my childhood on this mountain. He's leaning in, staring at the trunk of a young snow gum. The image would make a good portrait: Terry at the centre, everything else in the frame softened by the cold, wet mist.

I walk back, heart beating hard in my chest. It's a bright pink slug, moving up the trunk, leaving a glistening trail. Their waving tentacles are cream on the tips, the faint markings on the crimson body like the lateral veins of a snow gum leaf. When we lean closer, we see a tiny hole on their back, like a whale's blowhole.

I laugh but it's closer to crying. '*That* is a pink slug. This is the only place in the whole world where they live.' I shake my head. The lurid lolly-like colour, almost luminous, is so hard to believe.

'Have you seen them before?' Terry says.

'Never.'

Terry smiles, showing all his perfect white teeth.

'See their trails?' I point to the series of overlapping circles in wobbly lines etched into the bark. 'That's them feeding – on algae and bacteria.'

And then we see them. Dozens and dozens of pink slugs, sliding all over the wet mossy rocks and boardwalk.

'This is a good thing, right?' Terry says. His eyes are shining.

'It's a fucking *miracle*,' I say. 'We thought they were extinct.'

The slugs stop still, as if sensing us. We need to keep going but part of me is afraid to move, afraid of forgetting the details, of never seeing them again. Of no one believing us. Even Dianella would stop to photograph them. But I have no camera, no device.

'We have to go,' I say.

We walk slowly at first, not wanting to leave the moment behind. Terry keeps looking back, his mind working over.

'I spotted them,' Terry says. 'Me.' He taps his chest.

I smile. 'You did. And no one can ever take them away from you.'

His face is alight in a way I haven't seen in him before but recognise. 'We saw them together,' he says.

'Yeah.' And my voice cracks.

'I'll never forget this.'

'Have you learned about Black Summer?' I say. 'That first wave of firestorms on the east coast.'

'Yes,' Terry says.

'This mountain burned for weeks. Almost all the slug habitat went up. They thought they'd be gone, for sure. I mean, so vulnerable.'

'But they survived?'

I nod. 'When it rained, they came back. No one really knows how.'

'Maybe they hid under those rocks. Or in caves.'

'There are carnivorous snails, too,' I say. 'And glass snails. Only here, only on top of this mountain. Isolated for millions of years. Since this was all rainforest.'

'Glass?'

'You can see through their shells. All their insides, their heart.'

'Oh,' he says.

'I know, right. I feel like while they survive, maybe we can survive.'

Terry presses his lips together and lets out a lot of air.

When I look back, the mist has closed in, obscuring where we have been, as if it never happened.

'Do you think they know that they're on the brink of extinction?' Terry says.

I shrug my shoulders. 'Do we?'

He sighs. 'It must be lonely, don't you think?'

'I know what you mean.'

He turns, his eyes so clear and wide. 'Endlings,' he says. 'That's what they're called. The last of a species.'

'It's a good word,' I say.

༺

My parents saw pink slugs on their honeymoon. There were more pictures of slugs than of them. Every anniversary, when they came back to Kaputar, they walked for hours each misty morning, and even searched with headtorches at night. But they never saw them again.

They did see glass snails. Dianella's backlit shot, of the scrolling shell and outstretched tentacles, showed the shadow of the snail's heart just left of centre, like an ultrasound. She never exhibited that picture, but it was still the screensaver on her laptop last time I logged in. In the recording Dad made, you could see the snail's tiny pink heart, beating.

And I wonder if other beings can be a thin place, because something is shifting. I'm lightheaded, struggling to find my rhythm again. The air is so damp, droplets drip from my hair and nose. Ribbons of bark rattle all around us. The moss breathes.

A slug back from the brink, the delicate spiral of a snail's shell, like an unfurling fern frond. Like the Milky Way, our spiral galaxy, expanding in its own grand time.

What if the thresholds I long to cross are not portals to another dimension, but the capacity to fully inhabit our own? A way of circling back, into ourselves. Our best selves. What if we could see a way to make a new world, where all beings, no matter how fragile, could thrive?

01:31:20

THE JUNCTION WITH THE summit road is almost solid with people. The building excitement fizzes on my skin. But we're not heading for that high point. Those occupying the platform probably arrived days ago, and who knows what they paid for that privilege. The rest will be crammed into the top carpark and along the steps, probably climbing over the fence, out onto the knoll. We're heading in the other direction, for one of the viewing platforms looking south.

A willy wagtail lands on the edge of the tarmac and performs his dance, not perturbed by all the people. It almost feels as if other creatures are with us on this day, or we are more with them.

I've never had as many close animal encounters as when Dad died. Every time I went for a walk, it was as if the park had been repopulated with species. The baby wallaby hopping into my path and seeing me without startling. The fairy wren tapping at my window in the cabin. The yellow robin perching for a moment on the toe of my boot. The white-faced heron stalking for frogs within arm's reach. She registered me there but didn't alter her behaviour at all. It was tempting to see them as signs or guides, Dad's spirit returned. But I think it was that they had no fear of me, in that state, as if they recognised a wounded animal.

'Fin,' Terry says, pulling on my pack.

The Parks vehicle again. Coming up the road behind us, parting the sea of pilgrims.

Terry and I shift to the side of the road, trying to keep a group of uni students between us and them. The four-wheel drive crawls up the hill, windows down, until it's level with us. A ranger in an Akubra and sunglasses, her brown arm on the window ledge, looks in our direction. She says something to the driver and the vehicle stops. I hear Terry's intake of breath. My heart is pounding. Someone must have recognised Terry and called us in.

But two students rush to the window of the vehicle, blocking us from view. The crowd ahead is a swarm, moving in all directions. We step into it, a sea of people of all ages and descriptions. It reminds me of pushing through the cattle in the ATV. I pull my beanie down low and avoid eye contact. Bags, arms, hands, scarves all brush my body, jostling me this way and that. Voices swirl, perfumes, sweat, wool, beeps, tunes and tones from different devices, until even the slugs are blurred. I am blurred.

Terry pats his hand on my pack, as if to bring me back. I glance towards the cabins my parents honeymooned in but can only catch a glimpse around shoulders and heads. Other people will be staying there, warming themselves by the fire, watching from the safety of their decks.

And then the crowd is thinning. I can see the edge of it, and we're through, to the other side.

I gulp in breaths and check the watch. We're under an hour now, and every second counts. I lead the final climb to the carpark and the signs at the trailhead. The crowds and their noise fall away, replaced by footsteps and birdcalls.

'Have you been in a bushfire? Like happened here,' Terry says.

'No. Why?'

'Images from you. Flames. So close.' He shudders.

I turn away, trying to stop the rush of smell and sound. 'It wasn't that sort of fire.'

After Ilse's immolation, I didn't want to know about adults' plans for violence, self-harm. I tried to ignore all the meetings, the marks and pins on maps, Stella dehydrating meals, Pete doing hill sprints with a full pack, Jade working out every morning and evening, unpacking and repacking her ultralight kit. When I saw Des and Blair unloading the crates marked explosives, I told myself they must be repurposed boxes. It was a kind of magical thinking.

We had enough to deal with at school: six suicides in three years. Two of them on the same day. The day after they announced the reef was dead. It wasn't like any of us had been there or seen it alive, but the scientist who volunteered to make the announcement had. Trying to save it had been his life's work. It wasn't all the tears in his voice, it was his *kindness*. The care he took in delivering the news, when we had all let him down.

The future we were facing, or the lack of it, was just too much for some kids. Hild and I were sick of wearing black, sitting in the back row of whichever stupid church it was. They were all the same, hard benches and coloured windows that didn't really let in the light. When Hild and I held hands and cried through those ceremonies, it was a promise that we would never do that to each other.

I hadn't buried my father then. My mother hadn't disappeared into her studio. And Hild hadn't been treated like a lab rat. Maybe that's what becoming an adult is: accepting loss and change – and choosing to go on. There is still so much beauty. And love. But that's why hope is so scary, because there is more yet that we could lose. My mother and the others have all been waiting for me to step up. And now I've been given that chance.

01:05:21

WE SLIP BETWEEN THE bollards onto the trail itself, and level ground at last. Terry makes that long expulsion of air that signals relief. The Parks' vehicle is through the crowd and heading up the road towards us again. We walk as fast as we can, without looking back.

There are fewer people on this side of the mountain. Only people who know the park and have been here before. People like me. But most of them arrived hours ago, if not days. They are already in position.

At the junction, I have another decision to make. Left will take us out to the rock tops, over the lava fields. It will probably be less crowded and there will be spots with the view we want. But Dianella said to line ourselves up with Mount Dowe. So I turn right, onto the circuit track, almost running now. Terry is puffing but keeping up.

The solidity of snow gums and mountain gums is a comfort, a reminder of the pink slugs, all the strange workings of the world. If we hadn't camped overnight in the Pilliga, we wouldn't be hurrying now. But then we might have missed Hild and not got onto the mountain at all. And if we hadn't taken the detour to avoid people, we wouldn't have seen the pink slugs. You can't just go back and change one decision without unravelling everything.

We tramp over the carpet of pale blossom raining down from the snow gums above. Two king parrots, bright red and green, are munching away, using their feet as utensils. They register us, not oblivious, but not concerned with the urgency of our mission, either. My skin and scalp are tingling. Whether it is coming from inside or out, or both, I don't know. The light is changing, the moon already shadowing the sun.

The old wooden bridge has been replaced by new metal, the railings cold to touch. Even I find it hard to walk without noise. Not that there is much point. Terry has such a heavy tread, like a swamp wallaby. The stringybarks absorb some of our sound, softer to walk through, even though they're not touching me, nor I them.

We clang across a section of steel platform over the first soak, and then we're skirting the edge of the forest again. I stride down the log steps, feeling the shift in texture, the roughness on my skin at the point where forest meets heath.

'You said your dad stayed home with you?'

'At first. Then he took a job at Murchison and Mum had to stay home for a while.'

'He worked on SKA-Low?' It was a massive array, a forest of metal trees listening for radio signals, pulling in data at terabytes per second. Dianella had always wanted to photograph it.

'Yes. Before it went live.'

'Is it true that MuX deliberately ignored the quiet zone?'

'Yes. Dad said that happened.'

'But your parents ended up working for them?'

'It meant we could move to Canberra. Be together. And they offered a lot of medical support.'

'This docking plate your parents designed. It can attach to live satellites?'

'Yes,' he says. 'What are you thinking?'

'Blair and Des used something similar.'

'Blair is the one who asked about it?'

'Yeah. He was in charge of a project de-orbiting defunct spacecraft parts, abandoned launch-vehicle stages and other debris. They used robotics to gather in the pieces, extract precious metals or reusables, and strip them of alumina. Then they'd fling the rest into Earth's outer orbit, so it would be pulled into our upper atmosphere and burn up on re-entry.'

Terry nods.

'Did you go inside the main telescope? At the park.'

'Yes.'

'Blair and Des used that control room during the day, when no one else was there.'

'And when no one would notice flaming objects in the sky,' Terry says.

'Exactly. I think they must want to get back in there. They'd have power, connectivity. They could link up with other telescopes. Communicate with others.'

Terry frowns. 'But they'd have to get past those soldiers first.'

'That's what I'm worried about.'

I head for a secret spot of Dianella's, a flat rock just off the trail, where a twisted tree between two rocks made a good foreground feature. We push through the teatree thicket, my pack snagging. A branch springs back and scratches my face, Terry mutters behind me. When we reach the clearing, I stop dead. A group of older tourists is gathered around a long table covered with a white cloth and set with linen serviettes, champagne glasses and a pair of top-of-the-line eclipse glasses at each place. A cork pops and the women, all in matching 'Total Eclipse of the Heart' hoodies, cheer. They turn to stare, as if we're the ones out of place.

Rather than retrace our steps, I hop from rock to rock, along the edge. Whether it's the sudden view to the south or the drop, I'm unsteady, lightheaded again. I lean out, to see how far we are from the official lookout and how many people are up there. When I reach for the binoculars, the rock under my boot shifts. I lose my balance and then overcorrect, failing to take into account the weight of my pack. I grab at a branch but I'm already lurching forwards, towards the drop. The rock I dislodged goes over, plummeting into the abyss.

I'm resigned to following it, to ending in failure. But then I'm wrenched upright. Terry has hold of the straps of my pack, leaning backwards, using his full body weight. I steady myself, turn and grab his arm, and step back to safety. I take a shaky breath.

'Are you okay?' he says.

'All good,' I say. 'Thank you.'

He shrugs like it was nothing, but stands a little taller.

We push our way back through the teatree to the path. Honeyeaters call the alarm ahead of us. Where the track opens up, there are scraps of tissue and toilet paper in the bush, buzzing flies. And the hum of people ahead of us.

When we reach the lookout itself, hundreds of people are crowded around the cairn and scattered over the lava flow. Two film crews, with multiple cameras on gurneys, are packed in next to each other. A photographer is fitting solar lenses to each of the cameras to capture this last partial phase.

I search for a spot on one of the edges, in the gaps, but there is not enough space and no cover. And when I look back to Kaputar, only the tip of the radio tower is in view. Does it really matter?

I still can't figure out why Dianella needs us to signal. She knows exactly how long the eclipse will last, unless she's worried the changes in the moon's orbit might have altered those timings. Even then, she'll be able to see the whole thing for herself. *Unless.*

Unless Dianella is inside the telescope, her attention focused on control panels and screens, delicate operations. Someone else will be outside, on the narrow catwalk around the dome. Jade or Pete, waiting for our signal.

'There's one more lookout,' I say.

Terry looks at my watch. 'Thirty minutes!'

'I know,' I say. 'But this isn't right.'

00:16:26

WE CROSS THE LAST soak. Bootprints either side of the walkway have flattened the sedges and reeds, left divots in the moss. I can hear the swarm up at the transmission towers, streaming live to however many stations and feeds, the low hum of a generator, someone making announcements over a loudspeaker, the pop of corks and waves of cheering. There must be some sort of exclusive event inside the enclosure.

We follow the path down to Eckfords Lookout, and along the elevated walkway designed to keep everyone's boots off the fragile herbfield that the crowd is tramping all over. When I look down, the golden stars are in flower: five yellow petals nested in strappy green leaves, stamens quivering, somehow still intact. Another good sign. Terry looks where I'm looking. It takes him a moment, but he sees them – and smiles.

Two families have set up their tents on the herbfield itself, right beneath the sign asking people to keep off it. Their kids are picking flowers, collecting them in a glass jar. Barefoot at least, but they're making a muddy mess. Half a dozen drones buzz overhead. It's a circus.

Another line of professional photographers occupies the platform at the end of the walkway: Nikon, Canon, Sony, Olympus, even an old Hasselblad. Their long lenses on heavy-duty tripods are all pointed at the sky, their kitbags open at their feet. Two of them have their backs to us, leaning on the rail, following the moon's progress through filtered binoculars. One of the younger photographers, purple and blue hair poking out from his beanie, has his eyes on a control panel. It's him flying the drone low along the cliffs. None of them have noticed us.

I step onto the platform, run along the inside edge, leap down onto a rock, and grip the platform's base to work my way around to the ledge below, where, at last, there is no one else. I shrug out of my pack and go back for Terry.

One of the photographers is frowning, checking her viewfinder to make sure we won't be in frame.

'Hey,' I say.

Her cheeks are pink, her black Canon beanie pulled down over her ears. 'You can't just go down there right in front of us. My sponsors paid premium for this site. We've been camped here for two days,' she says. 'I've hardly slept it's been so cold.'

'I'll bet,' I say.

She glances at Terry.

'Hello,' he says.

'Look, I just don't think it's safe down there, kid.'

It's exactly what Dianella would say. She doesn't care about us. She just wants a clear shot.

'There really isn't anywhere else,' I say.

While she's looking around, hoping that there is somewhere else, some way she can get rid of us, I turn to Terry. 'Jump,' I say. 'I'll catch you.'

And Terry, bless him, does jump. I manage to grab him and turn in one movement, staggering onto the rock shelf. When I recover my balance, Terry is on his own two feet. He follows me around the edge, holding onto the platform with one hand, the back of my fleece with the other, until we're safe on flat rock – in the path of the moon's shadow, directly below Mount Dowe, with the radio mast behind us.

This time it's Terry who raises his hand for a high five. 'We made it!' he says.

I slap his palm. 'Good job.'

'And, we have the best seat in the universe.'

'Oh my goodness. Was that a metaphor?'

Terry grins. 'I got it, right? I got it.'

He leans over the edge to gauge the drop and blows out air through pursed lips. The mist has cleared, exposing the full expanse of the Western Plains, far below. The extent of the gasfields and mines, great grey circles and craters left in the earth, extinguishes any joy. Between and beyond, what was farming land is scorched bare and dry, laid to waste.

And beneath it all, the Artesian Basin, as unknowable as space. I can sense it shifting, as the eclipse nears, drawn by the moon.

Terry steps back from the edge, removes his pack and tucks it tight against the rock behind us. I focus on the jagged blue line on the horizon that was once my home, hoping for some feeling that my mother and the others are safe. But there is only a fleeting image of Blair's broad back, sweat darkening the centreline of his shirt, at the side door of the main telescope. And maybe that's enough, because while he still has breath, I know he won't give up. He never lets anyone down.

And there are the signs and wonders of slugs and starflowers to cling to.

I can just make out the Forest Tower, vehicles spilling out from the campsite. I offer Terry the binoculars. 'See how far we've come,' I say. 'You can see the route we took.'

He scans the landscape with binocular vision, like a raptor.

I rummage in my pack for the headtorch, laser and voice recorder, and lay them out on the rock. I tuck our eclipse glasses in the chest pocket of my jacket, fit the filters on the binoculars to check the progress of the moon's shadow, almost across the sun.

'How long now?' Terry says.

'Six minutes. Have a look.'

He tilts his head up. 'Wow,' he says.

People talk about a total solar eclipse as if it's about the sun, but it's actually all about the moon. Of the hundred-and-fifty-odd moons in the solar system, only ours can produce a perfect solar eclipse. Earth is the only planet where the moon is the right size and the right distance from the sun to pass between it and Earth with such precise alignment that it casts a shadow. For now. The moon is slowly drifting further away. Eventually, she'll begin to appear smaller in our sky, until she's too small to cover the sun.

☾

Drones buzz overhead, like blowflies. They aren't allowed in national parks, but maybe they've been issued permits. Whenever Dianella came across one, she would just tell the owner to 'bring it down'. Her rage, and stolen shirt with a Parks logo, was usually enough to get rid of them.

A pair of wedge-tailed eagles soar overhead, one much higher than the other. There is no updraft; they have to beat their wings, which steals a little of their majesty. The female locks eyes on us. I see the shift of her head, the span of her wings, her upturned outer primaries, like fingers. And then, with a full-body rush, I feel *everything*. The sensation of air moving over each feather, the subtle difference from tip to quill. The long pinions holding me up, the slightest shift controlling my direction. The downy feathers ruffling around my legs, like trousers, tucked up against my body.

At the edges, the curvature of Earth, the dark shadow coming. And below, Kaputar, all her wrinkles and folds. All the people gathered there on the mountain. Terry and I, so small, on a rock at the edge of the world. And then I'm thrown back into my own body, seeing so much less with my own weak eyes, and feeling all the more with my own thin skin.

A drone climbs suddenly behind us. The eagle turns her head at the movement, that high-pitched whine so alien in this space. She trims and tucks her wings, and drops into a dive, plunging down in a blur of furious speed.

Her claws clutch at the whirring rotors, failing to grip but knocking it off course. A piece of plastic flies off and falls, spinning towards the ground below. The photographer behind us swears. He manages to bring the drone back under control and pull it in.

Terry is staring at me. 'Did you just …?'

'That was all her,' I say.

We watch the eagles soaring higher and higher, on a thermal that came from nowhere, moving away, until they pass out of view. Terry zips his fleece to his neck and rearranges his beanie. The breeze has cooled and it will only get colder during the eclipse.

'How long?' he says.

'Just a minute or two now,' I say.

He rubs his hands together and tucks them under his legs. I place a new tape in the recorder and stand to look back over the base of the platform, between booted feet and angled tripod legs, at the scene behind us.

'The crowd has swelled. Everyone is rugging up, putting on their glasses, making adjustments to their camera settings, their telescopes, holding their devices ready, all while keeping one eye on the sky. The air zips and crackles with energy. The expressions on their faces range from fear to hope, excitement to resignation.'

It's as if we've entered some sort of twilight zone. I can hear the difference in my own voice. I turn back and sit down, cross-legged, to wait. The recorder, still running, beside me. I hand Terry one pair of glasses and fit the others on my face.

'Okay?'

Terry nods. 'I know it sounds crazy, but I feel like I'm going to see my parents after this.'

'Me, too,' I say.

TRUE NIGHT

Mount Kaputar National Park

Gamilaraay Country

00:00:28

EVEN AFTER ALL THE effort of the journey, the promised spectacle, anticipation swelling every cell in my body, the day still looks much like any other: bright sun high in the blue sky, the breeze shifting the leaves of the trees, a waft of eucalyptus and blossom. It's hard to believe that anything is going to happen, that anything will change. That's how it has always been, Dad used to say, part of the trick of the human psyche: unable to believe what is coming, despite all the evidence showing it to be true. I'm starting to wonder if we got it wrong, if all our meddling has even messed up the eclipse. And then a chunk of the sun disappears.

The photographers behind us gasp. I hear them bending to their cameras, adjusting their lenses, their settings, taking the shot. The light is changing, the energy. I know that it's the moon moving in front of the sun, but we can't see the moon. It looks more like someone is fitting a lens cap over the sun.

The sun is waning, like a god falling to Earth, reduced to mortality. The blue of the sky is saturated indigo. All other colour, the pale cratered plains below, dim and disappear. Only the mountain remains in alpenglow.

The pictures my parents showed me of a total solar eclipse were always taken through a telescope or camera. A ghostly sphere surrounded by lace filigree, the fine detail of the sun's corona. Tricksy, artful images. Being *in* it, is a different thing entirely.

There is a black hole in the sky.

Birds and microbats wheel around, searching for somewhere to roost. Insects chirp and whir their evening song. Terry grips my sleeve.

Darkness races fast across the plains, towards us. It's the moon's shadow moving across the Earth's surface, a broad black cone. The path of totality. And with it, a terrible wind. We see it coming. We feel it. We know it will reach us, even on this high point. And still, when it hits, we scream.

The screaming is inside as well as outside, on our skin and in our minds and our organs, our hearts, saturating all our senses. I feel what Terry feels and he is no longer other to me, or I to him. Even the people behind us. Or any creature, above and below ground. I sense them, and them sensing me – in ways and on wavelengths that there are no words for. It's primal.

The light is wrong. And the dark isn't right either. It's tungsten, platinum, or some element not from Earth. Strange, rippling patterns move over our rock and the platform behind us. Then the sun disappears.

People all over the mountain are screaming. I'm no longer sure what's real. If anything in my life was ever real. Not as real as this. The boundaries and limits of the world are breached and broken. All light is extinguished, Earth's daystar blacked.

We remove our glasses.

Only a slender silver ring marks the place where the sun once was. The pearly glow of the sun's corona feathers around the black disc of the moon, a cluster of bright beads at its edge, an intense sparkle, like a diamond. Then the diamond transforms to ruby, and wispy pink streamers radiate outwards. It's beautiful – and terrible. Earth, Moon and Sun are revealed for all they are: giant spheres, locked in orbit. The universe is so, so large, and we are so small, just specks, and only here for a moment. *This* is totality.

Despite my determination not to cry, not to be weak, tears stream down my cheeks. Everything is pouring out of me, all at once. My grief for Dad, my mother, Hild, the First Peoples, this Country, all the forests and beings we have lost, our view of the stars.

We're at the centre of an eerie three-hundred-and-sixty-degree sunset. The wind in the transmission towers twists and twangs, like a metal orchestra. The crowd has stilled. Somewhere behind us, a man is sobbing. The bizarre twilight reminds me of Vernon's old film negatives. Not reversed, but everything in outlines and shadows, in black and white, as if we have been propelled back in time. Or forwards, carrying the weight of knowledge of the world's end. And it does feel like the end.

'Fin.'

Terry's eyes are glassy in the not-light. His face has been transformed – by wonder, by terror. When he looks at me, when our eyes meet, we're connected in the darkness. It's too much.

'The signal,' Terry says.

I've forgotten our final task.

I reach for the laser, flick it on, and point it upwards, sweeping back and forth in a cross, three times. There is muttering and cursing; I've spoiled the photographers' shots.

My light is answered with another light, floating above the forest. Someone is on top of the Forest Tower, relaying the signal: a great purple spiral projected into the sky. The same symbol we've seen everywhere: on flags, T-shirts, hats, wristbands, stickers – and tattooed on the soft skin of Hild's inner forearm. She's part of this, somehow.

The spiral signal, too, is answered. All across the Pilliga, relayed from fire tower to fire tower. Until a line of purple light leads all the way to the Warrumbungles. And then, above Mount Woorut, from the observatory: a flickering green glow shimmering upwards, like an aurora.

It's as if I'm breathing pure oxygen after days at altitude. My mother is alive. Alive and in action. Everything is in motion. Everyone is in place, exactly where they were meant to be. Someone has Dianella's black box, carrying it to safety. We are part of something, something epic.

A great pulse of bright white light explodes outwards from the observatory. There is no sound, not at first. Just a suck of air pulling back and then gusting forwards. And with it, a quickening, like the sea right before sunrise. A ripple of energy passes through mountain, through rock, through our bodies, to the greatwater far below, connecting everything. They have taken back the observatory.

Then another explosion, much bigger, at the power station. The towers topple and fall, the building beneath them crumbles and collapses. A mushroom cloud of smoke rises into the sky, flames take hold. A jet of methane ignites.

The lights of the town go out, section by section. And all the scattered lights on the plains below. Only the wrecked power station and the gas wells flare and flicker, like great campfires from the Dreaming. Saturn, Venus and Mars are bright, low in the sky. Betel is watching.

Terry takes my hand. The shock of it is just one current within a stream, a river.

I can see our tiny bodies, falling through stars, moving across the sky, as if Earth is accelerating, turning. Forwards or backwards, flying or falling, I don't know. We're interstellar, like particles of stardust and gas, floating free of space and time, exploding in light. So many stars. Past, present and future collapse into this moment and this moment expands into space.

Are we dead?

But my boots are still on the ground and I can hear Terry breathing, feel the warmth of his hand in mine. It is the stars who are falling. Thousands of them. They are falling to Earth like angels, tearing into flame.

I'm laughing and crying at the same time — hysteria, euphoria. At last, I understand. They're bringing down the satellites. They are bringing them *all* down. Blair and Des — and my mother. They're pulling them out of orbit and into Earth's gravity field, and they're burning up on re-entry. It's the greatest meteor shower in history, and the whole world is watching.

⸺

The shadow cone races away, as fast as it came. We put our glasses back on to watch. She emerges, just a blinding edge at first, misted with pink clouds. The sun is still there, still ours. The whole process is reversed, though it seems quicker now, sped up. The crescent sun is growing and growing. There is light, brightening, and then the sky is blue again. So very blue. As if we're seeing that colour for the first time. So very beautiful, that it hurts. We have to blink, though we don't want to miss a moment.

A robin calls, fooled by the false dawn, certain that day is here again already and that they have called it in. Thornbills chirp in the undergrowth, awake from their brief sleep. People in the crowd behind us are cheering, clapping and whooping, as if it was all a show put on for us. The noise ripples out, flows down over the mountain, over the Nandewar Range, out over the Western Plains.

The Thinning

Terry looks different. Or less different, somehow. But older. As I feel older. It was sixty-nine seconds without the sun, when time stopped – and it was everything. We are witnesses to the end of the world as we knew it. I can imagine dying, a world without us, and it's peaceful.

This *is* a death, but not for us. Not yet.

There is more. I feel it in my blood, in the waters of my body. The uncoiling from deep underground, as if that greatwater has awakened, in answer to the eclipse, to all that has fallen.

'Fin,' Terry says. 'Look.'

The water is coming up. Only a trickle at first, it rises and rises, moving as extraordinary bodies of water do, so slow that it seems gentle, but containing enormous force. It flows into the power station and gas wells, dousing their lights one by one, and then a few at time, and then the rest are extinguished all at once with a *whoof*. The water tumbles into mine craters, filling them, turning them into dams before moving on, spreading outwards, pooling on the surface, like a seasonal lake following once-in-a century rains.

The satellites are still falling, reflected in the silver surface. The greatwater is still expanding, until it occupies the space where the forest used to be, reclaiming the land, returning it to an inland sea.

When it reaches the Pilliga Forest, the still-beating heart of this Country, the water slows into shallows, trickling around trunks, spiralling over that red sandy soil. I feel it soaking in, as if through my own skin, now so porous. The dark-barked ironbarks and callitris drink their fill and stand tall.

The water creeps outwards, around Nandewar, towards the town, towards base camp. I imagine their screams, the panic, as people run for their vehicles, for the safety of the mountain.

Hild. I reach for my pack and start throwing things in.

'We can't get there in time,' Terry says. 'She did say that they were on the high ground.'

The satellites are still coming down. A fragment makes it through our atmosphere, falling across the sky, its flaming trail reflected on the water's surface. We feel and then hear the impact, the wave reverberating outwards, and the fire is doused.

The drones go silent all at once and plummet to the ground. One lands on the rock near us with a metallic *thwack*. The photographer climbs down onto a ledge even more precarious than ours to retrieve the parts, desperate for the precious memory card, his once-in-a-lifetime footage. The woman behind us is still filming, filming it all, as true photographers do. When I go to check the time, the watch has disappeared from my wrist.

The water is slowing, seeping back into the soil. The satellites are thinning, just a few falling at a time. The spell we have been under is lifting. Questions and curses start behind us: devices are failing, reception dropping out. There are shouts and screams from the enclosure around the towers. The crowd begins to move.

'We should get out of here,' I say.

I clip my pack closed, stand, and sling it over my shoulders. My skin is electric, all my emotions at the surface. Terry is ready, beside me. We scramble back around the edge of the platform. The photographers are packing up, thousands of dollars' worth of gear now vulnerable. But their movements are careful, to avoid mistakes, and to allow space for each another.

'Hey,' the young photographer says, her face gentle. She extends her hand, to help me up, and I take it.

'Thanks,' I say.

She grips Terry's wrist and lifts him onto the platform. 'Stay safe,' she says. And she's looking right at him when she says it.

We cross the herbfield. The sobbing man looks up as we pass, his pupils dilated, his cheeks wet. His legs seem rooted to the soil.

'Are you okay?' I say.

'It was so beautiful,' he says.

We leave him there like that. Some people are checking on those around them, touching a shoulder or an arm, encouraging them to pack up. Others are staring at their still-glowing screens: wanting to contact loved ones, find out what has happened off the mountain and all around the world, check bank accounts, superannuation funds, the stock market. But nothing is loading.

A young woman wraps a small child in her bright scarf, watching her partner, who has a device to his ear.

'Not even the emergency number works,' he says.

There are exclamations, expletives. Anger and fear swirl around us.

'Stay close,' I say.

'I'm right here.'

We spring off the boardwalk and climb the log steps, dodging the strings of people streaming in from their vantage points. The snippets of conversation are disjointed and strange: worrying about parents, children, siblings, houses, vehicles, businesses, jobs, swearing they'll leave their old lives behind. As if we have a choice now.

The noise is coming from the enclosure. The special event people, thirty- and forty-somethings in suits and dresses, with bare arms and legs, are trapped inside. Empty champagne bottles and bamboo cups roll over the ground, coloured streamers snag on branches and clumps of grass, their colours already fading. The party people push at the wire fence, where the Spiral Helix crew are working to release the electronic mechanism on the gates.

'Let us out!'

'Fucking terrorists! What have you done?'

At last, the gates open and the suits and dresses rush out, in a wave of perfume and boozy fumes. I hold Terry back, letting them push and shove their way into the crowd ahead of us, starting a panicked rush to get away, down off the mountain.

The Helix mob are going the other way, into the enclosure. Two tall men in suits start shouting and throwing punches, trying to obstruct them – to pick a fight – but they're outnumbered and outskilled. Three tattooed Islanders bring the suits down, one at a time, in a gentle tackle.

A Helix team works at the base of the FM transmitter, patching in some sort of communication system with solar panels and a power bank. Long yellow leads run over the ground, to where an all-women film crew has set up on a rocky outcrop. The journalist's face and voice convey the euphoria we felt. The circle around her is growing.

Then we're carried by the crowd, only able to move forwards, with the flow. I keep a tight hold on Terry's pack, in front of me, as we surge past.

'It was the signal of a generation,' the journalist says. 'One woman daring to hold up a light.'

Terry turns to look at me over his shoulder.

I smile and shake my head.

The junction with the road down from the summit is a mass of humans trying to merge, like one of those all-way pedestrian crossings in the city. A woman stumbles on the uneven ground, her silver backpack knocking Terry over. He lands hard on the bitumen.

The woman stops and turns. 'Oh my god.' Her cheeks are red beneath a green hand-knitted beanie. She bends down to check on him.

'I'm fine,' he says, holding up his hands.

The woman helps him to his feet. 'I'm so sorry.'

'It's okay. Really,' he says.

And then she's gone, swept away by the tide of people.

We let them go, falling back to where there is no pushing and shoving, no hurry for the day to be over. Adults make room for the old and the very young. We're tender, seeing the world anew: the colours brighter, definition sharper, a greater depth of field. Terry and I move among others without the any of the apprehension we felt on the way up.

We walk on, one foot in front of the other, just two people in a mass of people, until the crowd spreads out, and we can walk side by side. Terry looks at me and smiles. Such a brave little smile. I drape my arm over his shoulder.

We came as pilgrims, and we leave as pilgrims. With nothing but what we carry on our backs, and the more generous for it. People gesture with a hand, make eye contact, smile. The buzz of the eclipse lingers. What we have shared is a bond that could knit us back together. We'll rebuild, somehow, with what we've learned, and things will be different.

Who knows what or where will be home, but we're going to find the ones we love: Hild and then Terry's parents.

I can feel my mother, not so far away, with the others. They'll find us. I know they will. And when they do, we'll be a family again.

The sun is going down in the west, the dams and lakes left behind on the plains reflecting silver. Soon we'll enter golden hour, and move through each stage of twilight, until we fall into the true dark of night.

The stars will all come out again, in their millions, bright and clear. The Milky Way, that wild river, will climb in our sky, twisting and expanding. The Dark Emu will fly overhead, shifting with the seasons. We have crossed over the threshold, wound back time.

The Dark Skies have returned.

Author's Note

Spelling of Gamilaraay/Gomeroi/Kamilaroi

I have chosen to use the longer spelling of Gamilaraay in *The Thinning*, because it was the form used in books I read early on and, to me, sounds most like the landscapes I describe. Others prefer the shorter form of Gomeroi.

There is no difference between 'k' and 'g' in most Australian languages. Some Europeans thought they heard 'g' at the start of the word Gamilaraay and wrote it down as Gummilroy, while others heard 'k' and wrote it down as Kamilaroi. This spelling was used to name the Kamilaroi Highway, and still features on road signage.

Linguists have since standardised the sound, using 'g' for all Gamilaraay words.

For more information, see: www.winanga-li.org.au/yaama-gamilaraay/kamilaroi-gamilaraay-or-gomeroi/

Santos Narrabri Gas Project

The fracking of the Pilliga Forest is not fiction. But it can still be stopped.

The Pilliga Forest spans half a million hectares in northern New South Wales and is one of the most important areas for biodiversity in eastern Australia. It is home to at least 300 native animal species, more than 900 plant species, and is the largest remaining area of native forest west of the Great Dividing Range.

The Great Artesian Basin is Australia's largest groundwater basin, and one of the largest bodies of underground freshwater

Author's Note

in the world. It lies beneath parts of the Northern Territory, Queensland, South Australia and New South Wales, spanning more than one-fifth of the continent.

Santos's $3.5 billion Narrabri Gas Project proposes drilling 900 coal seam gas wells across 95,000 hectares on Gomeroi land. Sixty percent of the area is Pilliga state forest. The project would require clearing 1000 hectares. The wells would descend more than a kilometre below the surface.

The gas project, and the associated pipeline project, have been met with strong resistance from the local Gomeroi community, farmers and environmental groups. A Gomeroi group, which applied for recognition of their native title in December 2011, has led a coalition opposing the gas project, arguing that fracking will pollute the Pilliga's waterways and the groundwater beneath it, including the Great Artesian Basin, contribute to climate change, and cause grave and irreversible consequences to Gomeroi lands and culture.

Fifty exploratory wells have already been drilled. In 2018, Santos sought approval to drill an additional 850 wells at 425 locations. New South Wales and federal governments at that time supported the project as part of Scott Morrison's 'gas-led recovery'.

The New South Wales Independent Planning Commission received more than 23,000 submissions. Almost 98 percent were opposed to the project, arguing that it could contaminate groundwater, lead to a loss of pressure in the Great Artesian Basin, affect biodiversity in the Pilliga forest, and release substantial greenhouse gas emissions. Climate scientist Professor Will Steffen has estimated the Narrabri Gas Project would produce more than 100 million tonnes of carbon dioxide over its 25-year lifetime.

In 2020, the Commission approved the Santos Narrabri Gas Project, subject to a number of conditions.

When the Gomeroi group and Santos failed to reach an agreement, Santos made several Future Act applications with the National Native Title Tribunal. A Future Act is a proposal to deal with land that affects native title rights and interests. Since its establishment in 1993, only a handful of decisions made by the Tribunal have come back in favour of First Nations people.

In 2022, the Tribunal approved the Santos gas project. The Gomeroi group appealed the decision in the Federal Court of Australia.

On 6 March 2024, in a landmark decision, the Federal Court of Australia ruled that the potential greenhouse gas emissions from the Santos Narrabri Gas Project were not adequately assessed in light of the Gomeroi Native Title claim. The court found that the negative impacts of the project would contribute significantly to climate change and fundamentally disrupt the rights of the Gomeroi people.

Santos is continuing to push ahead with the proposed gas project.

To find out more: Gomeroi Ngaarr: www.gomeroingaarr.org or email: info@gomeroingaarr.org; Lock the Gate: www.lockthegate.org.au

A percentage of author profits from the sale of *The Thinning* will go towards the community campaign against Santos.

Acknowledgements

This book was written on the unceded lands of the Gamilaraay, Wiradjuri and Walbunja peoples (Yuin Nation) – the original stewards and storytellers. I acknowledge their deep and continuing connection to Country and pay my respects to Elders past, present and emerging.

I'm thankful for Create NSW arts project funding, which made it possible to research and write this book.

I'm eternally grateful to my publisher at Hachette Australia, Rebecca Saunders, for her editorial insight and wholehearted support of *The Thinning* – and my writing in general. Thanks to David Winter for an insightful structural edit, Casey Mulder for a generous cultural sensitivity report, Libby Turner for the proofread, and Emma Rafferty for directing the process. Thanks also to my publicist, Alexa Roberts, and the whole team at Hachette Australia for bringing this book into the world and into the hands of readers.

Warm thanks to my agent, Jane Novak, for ongoing advice and support.

A special thank you to Barbara Simpson, once again, for the gift of a book: *The World at Night*, by Babak Tafreshi, which inspired the astrophotography thread for *The Thinning*. (And the very nice 14mm Sigma Art lens that has allowed me to apprentice myself to the dark arts.) Thanks also to David Magro for the 2023 Goulburn Astrophotography Masterclass, which set me on my way.

I'm particularly grateful to Peter Swanton, ANU, for the generous conversation around my early ideas and the world of cultural astronomy. Thanks to Professor Christopher Lidman and Dr Brad Tucker for granting me access to Siding Spring

Observatory after dark. And to John Whittall, NSW National Parks and Wildlife, for assistance planning my May 2023 research trip to Warrumbungle National Park, the Pilliga, Horton Falls National Park and Mount Kaputar National Park. Thanks also to Coonabarabran Stargazing for the well-storied tours of the AAT Observatory and Mount Woorut – and tips for the best photography spots after dark.

I'm grateful to Eleanor Limprecht for support finishing this book during a difficult time, feedback on the messy first draft, and the wounded animal line. My thanks to Lisa Traill for feedback and discussion of early drafts, the change in texture line – and all the textures of all those shared landscapes.

The Thinning was inspired and informed by many other books:
Astronomy: Sky Country, by Karlie Noon and Krystal De Napoli. Thames and Hudson, 2022.
The First Astronomers: how Indigenous Elders read the stars, Duane Hamacher and elders. Allen & Unwin, 2020.
Dr Space Junk vs The Universe, Alice Gorman. NewSouth, 2019.
The World at Night, Babak Tafreshi. White Lion Publishing, 2019.
An Immense World: how animal senses reveal the hidden realms around us, Ed Yong. Penguin 2022.
Becoming Animal: an earthly cosmology, David Abram. Vintage, 2010.
Solaris, Stanislaw Lem. Penguin, 1961.
Thin Places: a natural history of healing and home, Kerry ní Dochartaigh. Allen & Unwin Canongate, 2022.
The Moth Snowstorm: nature and joy, Michael McCarthy. John Murray, 2015.

Acknowledgements

The Mother Fault, Kate Mildenhall. Simon & Schuster, 2021.

Ways of Being: beyond human intelligence, James Bridle. Penguin, 2022.

The Darkness Manifesto: on light pollution, night ecology, and the ancient rhythms that sustain life, Johan Eklöf (trans. Elizabeth DeNoma). Scribner, 2020.

Our moon: a human history, Rebecca Boyle. Sceptre, 2024.

I've read many accounts of total eclipse experiences, but *The Thinning* owes most to 'Total Eclipse' by Annie Dillard (1982), which I first read decades ago and have never forgotten. In particular, her image of a lens cap being fitted over the sun, which shaped some of the themes of my story.

The story of Mount Stromlo Observatory in the 2003 Canberra fires is drawn from Professor Brian Schmidt's experience, as related in Jarrah Aguera's 'Ashes under foot and heavens above: remembering Canberra's 2003 bushfire disaster', *ANU Reporter*, 18 January 2023.

Rambo the fox is a real story, widely reported. He has his own Wikipedia entry. My account is drawn from 'Fox on the Run' by Angus Fontaine (*Good Weekend*, 21 May 2022) and 'Rambo, the fox who outfoxed the hunters, bites the dust' by Tracey Ferrier (*Sydney Morning Herald*, 14 March 2023).

Inga Simpson terrifies and enthralls with this truly remarkable novel of a woman who must face her worst fears to survive and find beauty in a world under attack.

Fear is her cage. But what's outside is worse...

It's night, and the walls of Rachel's home creak in the darkness of the Australian bush. Her fear of other people has led her to a reclusive life as far from them as possible, her only occasional contact with her sister.

A hammering on the door. There stand a mother, Hannah, and her sick baby. They are running for their lives from a mysterious death sweeping the Australian countryside – so soon, too soon, after everything.

Now Rachel must face her worst fears to help Hannah, search for her sister, and discover just what terror was born of us... and how to survive it.

OUT NOW